"A masterful mystery writer."
—Chica

PRAI
GOING NO

"*Going Nowhere Fast* is a dizzying and hilarious escape from seriousness . . . sidesplitting . . . Even more impressive is how the versatile author, a father of two, so convincingly speaks in the voice of a mother of five. Wry, wise, tough, and, when the occasion demands it, credibly sentimental, Dottie is one of the most lovable fictional mothers around. I started missing her as soon as I closed the book."
—*New York Times Book Review*

"Haywood has created the freshest and funniest pair of sleuths to grace the genre in a long while. Despite the hilariously wicked plot, there's nothing coy about Dottie and Joe. They're acerbic, insightful, compassionate—and consistently charming. I definitely want to be wherever their Airstream next takes them."
—**JOAN HESS**, author of
Tickled to Death and the Maggody series

"Mothers are the most maligned figures in life and literature. But thanks to Gar Anthony Haywood's new protagonist, women with children have a voice: witty, persevering Dottie Loudermilk, mother of five dysfunctional grown-up kids and the wife of a man in love with his Airstream. Haywood has created a wise, compassionate character. All right, so Mr. Haywood is a man. But God, he knows his women."
—**MELODIE JOHNSON HOWE**, author of
The Mother Shadow and *Beauty Dies*

This edition includes a special preview of Gar Anthony Haywood's *Bad News Travels Fast*, featuring Joe and Dottie Loudermilk, available in hardcover from Putnam.

MORE PRAISE FOR
GAR ANTHONY HAYWOOD

YOU CAN DIE TRYING

"A masterful mystery writer ... Not everyone can tell a story in the way it should be told. Gar Anthony Haywood is just such a writer and one deserving of greater attention by the book-buying masses ... Aaron Gunner [is] a unique and important voice ... Haywood's the real thing, all right, a formidable artist with something important to say about some of the most troubling issues of our day. And he tells a good story."

—*Chicago Tribune*

"Grim accuracy and emotional insight ... a rousing, satisfying, cinematic ending ... Beyond his skills as a story-plotter (ingenious in this case), Haywood's strength is to capture so well and perceptively a time, a place, and a likable protagonist in tough circumstances."

—*Los Angeles Times*

"Tightly plotted with a satisfyingly tricky conclusion ... Excellent reading."

—*Booklist*

"Gunner is a rarity in recent detective fiction: soured, yet utterly believable, tough and resourceful without being cartoonishly overblown. This pulsating mystery strengthens an already forceful series."

—*Publishers Weekly*

"Haywood's freshest, leanest yet."

—*Booklist*

GOING NOWHERE FAST

Gar Anthony Haywood

BERKLEY PRIME CRIME, NEW YORK

GOING NOWHERE FAST

A Berkley Prime Crime Book / published by arrangement with the author

PRINTING HISTORY
Putnam hardcover edition / August 1994
Berkley Prime Crime edition / October 1995

ISBN: 0-425-15051-8

Berkley Prime Crime Books are published by
The Berkley Publishing Group,
200 Madison Avenue, New York, NY 10016.
The name BERKLEY PRIME CRIME and the BERKLEY PRIME CRIME design are trademarks belonging to Berkley Publishing Corporation.

PRINTED IN THE UNITED STATES OF AMERICA

10 9 8 7 6 5 4 3 2

For my nana, Pilar Ray,
whose love made all things possible

ACKNOWLEDGMENTS

The author is deeply indebted to the following people whose generous contributions of time and expertise made this book possible:

Ken Eckley, President, Region XII,
Wally Byam Caravan Club International, Inc.

Joyce Vaughn, Grand Canyon National Park Lodges

David R. Swickard, Law Enforcement Specialist,
Grand Canyon National Park

John Beaver, Thor Industries, Inc.

Russ Burklund, TVETEN RV Company

And the CompuServe Commandoes:

Bob Zambenini

Larry Hewin

Carol Meredith

We thought we had lost Bad Dog in Las Vegas.

He had followed us there from California, acting on a wild hunch, and come upon us as we were watching all the wrong numbers light up on the keno board at Bally's. He reeked of all the usual odors, liquor and sex and low-grade motor oil, and looked like he hadn't had a square meal in over a month. Naturally, he was also broke, and was counting on Big Joe and me to carry him for the weekend. Joe decided early on that we would kill him and bury his body out in the desert somewhere, well off the highway so that it might never be found, but I voted that idea down, though it did have a certain appeal. Eventually, all we did was let Dog make a nuisance of himself all day Saturday and Sunday, then ditch him bright and early Monday morning. We were probably halfway to New Mexico by the time he woke up in the mirrored motel room we had dumped him in the night before.

We thought that was the end of him.

Then one day, eight months later, he turns up again, at a state-operated trailer park on the south rim of the Grand Canyon in Arizona. He was waiting for us at the back of a dark closet, with a gun in his right hand and an empty can of Budweiser in his left. I pulled the closet door open and there he was, hunched over uncomfortably beneath a canopy of hanging clothes, his eyes wild with anticipation and his grip on the gun unsteady. He was still heavy with baby fat and his hair was as unruly as ever, a dark brown tumbleweed someone had glued to his head, and when he saw me, he grinned, just like a little boy, and belched extravagantly.

"What's up, Moms?" Bad Dog asked.

Knowing full well how much I hate it when he calls me that.

1

"You left the door open again, didn't you?" Big Joe asked me. I could almost feel his loving hands closing around my throat.

"Yo, Pops," Bad Dog greeted his father cheerfully, stumbling out of the closet toward him. One of Joe's favorite polo shirts was tangled hopelessly around his left ankle.

"I'm not talking to you. I'm talking to your mother," Big Joe said.

"Cool. I'll just go in the kitchen an' get me—"

"You go near that refrigerator, boy, and I'll drop you like a bad habit!"

The threat froze Dog dead in his tracks. The child is slow, Lord knows, but he isn't stupid.

Joe regarded him a moment, daring him to move, then turned his gaze on me again, making a show of crossing his arms in front of his chest. He's a big, handsome man of fifty-two, my husband, bronze-skinned and bald like an eagle, and when he strikes this particular pose, the muscles in his forearms defy you to tell him the slightest thread of untruth. I smiled and shrugged. "I thought I locked it, baby," I said sweetly.

Sometimes the "baby" helps in situations like this, sometimes it doesn't.

"You always say that. 'I thought I locked it.' You're gonna wait until you get us both killed, woman. Just keep it up."

The "baby" hadn't helped.

"If you're talkin' 'bout the gun," Bad Dog said, trying to defend me, "it ain't even loaded."

He waved the weapon in his hand around like a harmless grapefruit, just to prove the point.

Only now did he realize his mistake: Big Joe hadn't even noticed the gun before now.

"Waitaminute, waitaminute. A *gun?* You brought a *gun* in here?" my husband asked him, in total disbelief.

Bad Dog didn't say anything.

"You brought a gun into *my house?* Have you lost your mind?"

Now, there were a number of ways our son could have responded to this question, of course. Some of them smart, some of them not so smart. Bad Dog's options were unlimited—and yet, from among them all, he chose the absolute worst of the lot. For rather than accept the well-intentioned—though admittedly mind-numbing—lecture his father was about to bestow upon him with all the grace common sense should have dictated, he looked Big Joe right in the eye and, with total irreverence, told him, "This ain't no 'house.' It's a Winnebago."

And with that, I closed my eyes and began to pray. Out loud.

Because the boy was doomed now, without a doubt. He had taken his mindless insubordination too far. Men

always have their limits, as any woman can tell you—
personal lines of demarcation they are forever defying
others to cross—and Dog had just crossed one of his
father's. For Elvis, the primary rule of thumb had been,
tread lightly around the fancy blue shoes on his feet; for
Joseph Loudermilk II, as of a full year ago anyway, the
rule is, never—*ever*—refer to our trailer home as a
"Winnebago." For he and I did not sink $40,000 of our
hard-earned retirement money thirteen months ago on
anything quite so ordinary as that. We are the owners
of an *Airstream*—a beautiful, colossal, luxurious silver
god on wheels—and we are damn proud of it. Cedar-
lined wardrobes, a queen-size bed, double porcelain
sinks, four-burner range with oven, a pull-out pantry,
microwave oven—the *works!*

Not that our children have ever understood the difference, of course. They like to think we've lost our
minds. When they first heard of our intentions to purchase an Airstream, and what we consequently meant to
do in it, Delila accused us of being senile, Walter wanted
to take us to court, Edward claimed our doctors were
guilty of overprescribing, and Theodore—known to his
parents and older siblings alike as Bad Dog ever since
he celebrated his second Christmas by leaving a Yuletide
log of his own making beneath the family tree—insisted
we had fallen in with a religious cult. Only Mo, our
oldest and most consistently sensible offspring, seemed
to have any appreciation whatsoever of the path we had
decided to take in retirement.

Fortunately, Big Joe and I didn't give a hoot.

We had made up our minds, together, that we were

not going to live out the rest of our lives in the conventional, turtle-on-its-back manner of most retirees. No thank you. Big Joe had no affinity for shuffleboard and I had no patience for bridge. So we came up with a more stimulating scheme for our remaining time together: We were going to hit the open road and never look back. Buy ourselves a land yacht and see every inch of the world we could find with a broken yellow line running through it. Vacationing somewhere in Europe once a year sounded like fun, sure, but this promised to be more exciting, and for months at a time, not just a few days or weeks. Discovering America, mile by incredible mile—that was the new Loudermilk manifesto. And no one was going to talk us out of it.

No one.

Big Joe only spent one weekend trying to explain this to our children, then he shut up. He just pulled our brand-new Ford pickup truck and twenty-four-foot Airstream Excella into the driveway of the house we'd sold only two weeks before and told everybody good-bye—after introducing us all, that is, to a long-winded song of praise and hype we have since come to know and dread as "The Battle Hymn of Jackson Center, Ohio."

Jackson Center, Ohio, you see, is the home of Airstream, Incorporated, and the Hymn is a seemingly interminable sales pitch for the brand Joe apparently inherited, word for word, from a salesman named Bucky Overton out at World on Wheels, the recreational vehicle dealership in Long Beach where Big Joe bought our trailer home. Watching my husband recite this epic paean is akin to watching a virgin bride recite her wedding vows, and I should know; I've seen and heard him do it more than a hundred times since that first fateful day of ownership. Joe raises his gaze skyward, speaks the hallowed name in breathless, awe-inspired tones—*Airstream*—and then cuts loose with a long and unvarying list of the brand's most admirable qualities, as in state-of-the-art aerodynamics; a distinctive, polished aluminum skin; and unbeatable American craftsmanship.

In a word, *class*.

Over the last thirteen months, I have learned to take our Airstream ownership very seriously, but for Big Joe, faith in the Airstream name has become a religion, leaving him convinced that anything else calling itself a *trailer home* is just a laughably inferior pretender to the classification. An Airstream is a *home* that just happens to have wheels for a foundation, Joe likes to say, and anyone who doesn't realize this—who lacks the insight necessary to distinguish a true home from a rolling bungalow of some other make and model—is a fool. A fool, in fact, who must be looking for a fight.

No one knows this any better than Bad Dog. He's heard the Battle Hymn himself at least a dozen times, more than all of our other children combined. And yet, there he stood: foot firmly planted atop one of his father's most cherished pieces of clothing, armed like Dirty Harry, referring to Lucille—the name Joe bestowed upon his most prized possession our first week on the road—as a *Winnebago*.

And people wonder why some animals eat their young.

"What'd you say, boy?" Big Joe asked Dog, edging

ominously forward toward him.

"I said I gotta go to the bathroom," Bad Dog said.

I told you the child isn't stupid.

"So what's stopping you?"

"Well, you know. The dead guy."

"What?"

"There's a dead guy on the toilet. Don't tell me you didn't know?"

"*Jeez Looweez,* Dottie," Big Joe said, screwing his face up in disgust before turning it toward me. "This boy's come in here on some kind of *trip!* I've been drinking Budweiser for forty years, and I haven't *once* seen any dead people sitting on the toilet!"

"Hey. Look for yourself," Bad Dog insisted. "Man's got his pants down round his ankles and everything."

Joe had no intention of looking for himself, of course, so I did it for him. Dog's story was just too imaginative for a child who never received a grade higher than a C− on an English paper to make up. I turned to the bathroom door behind me and slid it open all the way. Dog and his father just stood there behind me, peering over my shoulders. And guess what.

"See? What'd I tell you?" Bad Dog asked.

"You ever see this man before?" Park Ranger Will Cooper asked us again, referring to the dead, middle-aged white man perched atop our chemical toilet.

"No. Never," I said. Cooper, Big Joe, and I were standing just outside the open bathroom door as a second park ranger looked the corpse over, scratching the side of his head and trying to keep a smile from taking over his face. We were all grouped together in the narrow space between Lucille's bathroom and closet door, fighting a common feeling of claustrophobia that Joe and I were ordinarily immune to.

"You sure?" Cooper asked.

"Yes."

"Maybe if you took another look at him—"

"She doesn't need another look at him," Big Joe cut in, snarling. He was not a jealous man by nature, but I could tell he was growing less and less tolerant of the way Cooper kept addressing most of his questions to me. Frankly, I had begun to wonder a little about that myself. "We don't know the man. How many times do we have to say it?"

Cooper showed my husband a smile, as thoroughly professional as it was condescending. The young man had a huge red mustache that spilled over his top lip like an overfed Chia pet, and bright, energetic eyes. He put his pen and notepad down and said, "This is tedious for you, I know, Mr. Loudermilk. But this *is* a homicide we're dealing with here, and, as there was no identification on the body . . . Well, you being a former law enforcement officer yourself, I'm sure you can understand why I have to ask these questions more than once."

I liked the way the red mustache wiggled when he talked.

"Okay. So I understand," Big Joe said. "But that doesn't change the fact that we've told you everything we know. At least a dozen times. We don't know who that man in there is, we don't know what he was doing using our bathroom, and we sure as hell don't know who killed him before he could finish. My wife left the damn door open when we went out for our daily run, just like we said, and the Thinker was there when we got back, exactly as you see him. We never touched a thing.''

"And your business here today is strictly recreational. Is that right?''

"Of course. We're just tourists visiting the park like everybody else.''

"And him? What about him?''

"Who? Theodore?''

"Yes sir.'' Cooper was looking at Bad Dog like something rancid he had found in his refrigerator. Our son was sitting up at Lucille's front end watching Oprah on television, one hand submerged in a bag of potato chips, the other clamped around a fresh can of his father's beer. He didn't seem to have a care in the world.

"What about him?''

"He didn't know the deceased either. Is that your understanding?''

"Yes. It is. I heard him tell you that himself, not five minutes ago.''

"Yes sir, but—''

"It's the truth, Officer Cooper,'' I said flatly. "Theodore never saw that man before in his life.'' It was what he had told us before the ranger's arrival, and I believed him. Dog can tell his father any lie and never flinch, but he always falls apart when he tries to lie to me. In that sense alone, he is a mother's dream.

Cooper gazed at me and smiled. His mustache twitched to the right. "Yes ma'am,'' he said.

Out of the corner of my eye, I could see the crown of Big Joe's hairless head turning red, like the burner on an electric stove coming slowly to life.

"Look—" he said to Cooper, just as the door to our trailer opened and a fat man toting a heavy black leather case stepped inside to join us. I could hear Lucille's suspension groan a mild complaint beneath his additional weight.

"Ah. Henry," Cooper said. "Glad to see you could make it."

"Where is he?" Henry said, apparently in no mood for amenities, huffing and puffing as he dabbed at his face with a giant white handkerchief.

"In there. He's all yours," Cooper said, gesturing toward the bathroom.

"You did have the decency to flush the toilet, I hope."

The ranger just looked at him.

"Aw, damn," Henry said. "This job of mine isn't revolting enough, is that it?"

Cooper grinned. "Relax, Henry. The bowl's clean. Either our man got shot before he could get his engines started, or the killer propped him up on the seat as a gag."

"Hmph. Some gag. What the hell's this world coming to, sitting a stiff up on a toilet's supposed to be a gag?" Without waiting for an answer, Henry took a deep breath, squinched up his nose, and started toward the bathroom, shimmying like a bowl of Jell-O to slip past us along the narrow corridor.

"Excuse me," Cooper said to Joe and me, tipping his

hat in my direction before trailing after the man we could only assume was the county coroner.

Big Joe immediately took my arm, scowling, and led me a few feet away, trying to get us out of our visitors' earshot.

"All you had to do was lock the door this afternoon," he grumbled. "Just lock the door, like I've asked you to do a thousand times. But nooooo . . ." He shook his head from side to side.

"I'm sorry, Joe. What more can I say?"

"We're going to be here forever, now, you know. They're not going to let us go anywhere until they find out who this man was, and who killed him."

"So?"

"So I'd only planned for us to be here long enough to *see* the Grand Canyon, Dottie. Not long enough to *refill* it. We were going to—" He caught himself, remembering our son on the lounge nearby, and lowered his voice to just above a whisper. "We were going to move on to the southeast Friday, remember?"

"We still might. Think positive," I said.

"Hmph. They're going to take Lucille away. You watch."

"Oh no. They wouldn't do that."

"They wouldn't, huh? This is a crime scene, Dottie. They have lab tests to run. And I'd be willing to bet they don't have the facilities to run 'em here at the park."

Suddenly, I was all out of optimistic reassurances.

"But then, maybe if you talked to the boy, he'd cut us some slack and just let us go. What do you think?"

He had lost me, and my face must have shown it.

"You gonna stand there and tell me you haven't noticed how sweet he is on you?"

"Who?"

"Your friend Cooper back there. That's who. Three hundred women in this park under thirty, and he's in here makin' goo-goo eyes at a fifty-three-year-old mother of five. I ought to slap those overgrown nosehairs right off his face!"

"I don't know what you're talking about," I said, starting to laugh.

"And *you*. Woman, you act like you've never seen a mustache before."

"What?"

"You trying to deny it? That your eyes weren't glued to the man's upper lip every time he opened his mouth?"

"Joe, that's ridiculous."

"It might be ridiculous, Moms," Bad Dog said, inviting himself into our conversation, "but it's the truth. I noticed it too." He shrugged apologetically at me, grinning from ear to ear.

Big Joe suddenly noticed the can in his son's hand and rushed to the refrigerator, yanking the door open. "Boy! That was my last beer! You know that?"

Bad Dog stuffed his mouth with a handful of potato chips and mumbled his latest weak apology.

2

Big Joe was right, of course. We were stuck at the Grand Canyon.

They had been extremely apologetic about it, but the two plainclothes detectives from the Coconino County Sheriff's Department who eventually showed up to take over the murder investigation from Ranger Cooper rendered us all but prisoners on the park grounds. We weren't under suspicion of anything, they said, but for several days, at least, we were going to have to stay right where we were. I had hoped this was only because they wanted us available for further questioning, but that was just wishful thinking.

"Sorry, folks, but we're going to have to impound your trailer," the detective named Crowe had said.

They told us they were going to have to take her down to Flagstaff to run some lab work on her, just as Joe had predicted, and we'd be without her no longer than three or four days, tops. I myself took the news badly, but it broke my heart to see the effect it had on Big Joe. It was as if they had told him they were going to tow me down to Flagstaff instead.

A small crowd of curious onlookers, having already

witnessed the removal of a corpse from our trailer by several employees of the county coroner's office, watched as a pair of deputy sheriffs hitched Lucille up to a mustard-yellow Chevy truck with Coconino County badges on the doors, showing great restraint as Big Joe supervised the entire operation. While my husband snapped orders and mumbled complaints outside, driving Detective Crowe to distraction, Bad Dog and I removed a mere handful of belongings from Lucille under the watchful eye of Crowe's partner, Detective Bollinger, who inspected everything we collected with professional suspicion.

Then they took Lucille away.

Big Joe took my hand as we watched her vanish into the distance, her gleaming silver body rolling gently from side to side with each dip in the dirt road. I would say it was like watching one of our children pack up and leave home for good, except that Joe and I had always been tearfully ecstatic on those occasions. Suffice it to say that it was a difficult thing for us to do, Bad Dog included.

And so it was that we became the guests of the Bright Angel Lodge, one of the more historic and colorful hotels situated in the park proper, courtesy of the Coconino County Sheriff's Department. They gave us a lovely cabin with a fine view right on the rim of the Canyon, and the staff there treated us with great kindness, but all of this was wasted on Joe. Stripped of both his beloved trailer home and his freedom of movement, he couldn't have been any more miserable had they locked us all up in an outhouse.

"Damn, Dottie," he kept saying, over and over again.

"I know, baby," I would reply.

"If you'd just locked that damn door—"

My "baby"'s still weren't doing squat.

Finally, exasperated, I told him, "Look. Why don't you try looking at the bright side of all this for a change?"

"The bright side? *What* bright side?"

"Well. For starters . . ." I had to come up with something fast, so I said, "This is all very exciting, isn't it? I mean, when you really stop and think about it?"

"Exciting? You call finding a dead man growing stiff in your bathroom exciting? Are you insane?"

"Coming from someone who used to think crime was the most thrilling thing on earth, Joseph Loudermilk, that's an awfully odd question to ask, isn't it?"

"What?"

"You heard me. And you know precisely what I'm talking about, too."

"I do not."

"Oh yes you do."

"I said I don't!"

"And I say you do."

"Listen. If you're trying to suggest I'm turned on by all this just because I used to be a cop, you can forget it. I've been retired from police work for over two years now, and that's just the way I like it."

"Is that so?"

"Yes, that's so."

"Just because a man's retired from something, Joe, doesn't mean he doesn't miss it," I said.

"So I miss it. So what? You do something for twenty-five years, you can't help but miss it a little when it's gone. But miss it enough to want it back?" He shook his head at me, grimacing at the thought. "No, Dottie. Not now, not ever."

"Joe, the man died in our trailer. Sitting on your favorite reading chair. Don't you think we're entitled to find out how and why, if we can?"

"No, I don't. I don't *want* to know the how or the why of it. It's none of my business, and it's none of yours, either. But I can tell you *one* thing." He turned his head in the direction of our son, who was camped in front of the TV in our room, absently watching a basketball game while spraying Oreo cookie crumbs all over the carpet. "If it were, I sure as hell know who I'd ask about it."

"Who? Me?" Bad Dog asked his father innocently.

"You're damn right, you. What the hell are you doing here, anyway? Who told you where to find us? And how the hell'd that dead white man end up in our house?"

There was that word again: *house.* I held my breath and waited to see if Dog's last brush with death had taught him anything at all.

"I told you. I don't know nothin' about that man. He was in the bathroom when I came in, just like you found 'im."

"Dead."

"That's right."

"And you didn't shoot him."

"No! My gun wasn't loaded! And it hadn't been fired, either. You said so yourself, remember?"

He had Joe there. Inspecting Dog's gun was the first thing my husband had done after we found the body, and he'd told us both afterward that the weapon was clean.

"That doesn't mean you couldn't have used something else to shoot him," Big Joe argued. "If you're crazy enough to bring one gun into my house, you're crazy enough to bring a dozen."

"I didn't shoot the man, Pops. I didn't even know 'im."

"Then what the hell were you doing in the closet?"

"I was hidin'. What else? I heard you guys comin', and I thought it was the killer, returnin' to the scene of the crime. That's what they always do, right? Return to the scene of the crime?"

Big Joe didn't answer him.

"All right, Theodore," I said. "Your father and I believe you."

Joe made a face and directed it at me, but he remained silent.

"Now. Your father asked you how you found us."

Bad Dog nibbled on his Oreos and fell silent, just like his father.

"Did Mo tell you where we were?"

"Nobody told me nothin'," Dog said, in his inimitable double-negative style. I spent twenty-two years trying to break him of the annoying habit, but alas, *I didn't never have no luck.* "I found out where you guys were on my own."

"How's that?" Big Joe demanded.

Dog shrugged. "I saw a letter."

"What kind of letter? And stop dropping those cookie crumbs all over the carpet!"

"It was just a letter. Addressed to you. I don't know what was in it." He started brushing the crumbs he'd littered the floor with in all directions, as if by dispersing them throughout the room he could make them disappear.

"Where did you see this letter, Theodore?" I asked him, tired of listening to him dance around his father's questions like a mob boss facing a grand jury.

He looked at me, his eyes wide and helpless. He knew the truth was about to emerge from his lips, and there was nothing he could do to stop it.

Sometimes, motherhood makes you feel like you've got every man on the planet by the short hairs. It's great.

"At Mo's," Bad Dog said.

"At Mo's?"

"Yes ma'am." He nodded to make sure I believed him.

Mo is what we all call Maureen, Dog's oldest sister. Mo is a tax attorney who lives in La Jolla, California, a USC grad and mother of two, and she takes care of all Joe's and my business affairs. Our bank accounts, our travel reservations, our medical bills—Mo handles everything, and under the strictest code of silence. No one knows our itinerary but her. No one else needs to know. (If I haven't yet made this abundantly clear, all our other children are pains in the derriere, for a vast assortment of depressing reasons, and when Joe and I left California, we didn't exactly leave them behind by accident.)

"What were you doing at Mo's?" Big Joe asked.

"I wasn't doin' nothin'. Just sayin' hello."

"Uh-huh."

"I can't go visit my sister if I want?"

"No. You wanna talk to your sister, make a phone call. Or write her a letter. Anything you have to say to her in person can wait until Christmas."

"Joe—" I said.

"Joe nothing. Only reason this boy went out to La Jolla was to find out where we were. You know it, and I know it. And if I have to tell you why, Dottie, you haven't been paying attention."

"I don't need any money," Bad Dog said, insulted.

"Boy, don't give me that. You *always* need money."

"Okay, so I could use a few dollars. But that ain't the only reason I wanted to see you."

"So what's the other reason?" I asked him, no doubt taking the words right out of his father's mouth.

"Wait a minute, Dottie," Big Joe said. "I wanna hear what he means by 'a few dollars,' first."

"Moms, it's like this," Dog said, deciding to ignore his father's presence in the room altogether. "All I need is a thousand dollars and a ride to Pittsburgh."

"*Pittsburgh?*" I cried.

"*A thousand dollars?*" Big Joe howled.

"What? You can't handle that? A thousand measly bucks and a little detour along your way?"

I leapt to my feet to block my husband's charge, stopping him before he could get up a head of steam, and said, "Joe, if we kill the child now, we'll never find out what he's talking about."

"I don't care what he's talking about. Whatever it is, it's gonna cost me a thousand dollars, and that's all I need to know about it!"

"Theodore," I said, turning to face Bad Dog again, but keeping myself between him and his father, "what in heaven's name is in *Pittsburgh?*"

"A job, Moms," he said. *"The* job. The one I've been waitin' for all my life."

So that was why he'd been refusing work all these years. He'd been waiting for *the* job.

"What kind of job?"

"You ain't never gonna believe it," he said.

"That much we know," Big Joe said.

Ignoring him, Dog pointed to the familiar logo on his dingy T-shirt and said, "I'm gonna work for the Raiders. I got me a job with the Silver and Black!"

"What?"

The Los Angeles Raiders are, to the best of my knowledge, a professional football team, and they have always been Joe's favorite. (Why men even claim to *have* a "favorite" football team, I'll never understand, because they'll watch any two teams play a game to the final gun no matter how little they care for either one. It's the *game* men are addicted to, sisters, not just a franchise or two, so don't let the warm-up jackets and bumper stickers fool you. Your man may profess to be a Seahawk fan, but he's going to watch the 0 and 15 Bengals play the 1 and 14 Colts under six feet of snow on the last day of the season, no matter what else you had planned for him.)

"The Raiders?" Big Joe asked skeptically.

"That's right. The Silver and Black Attack! Commitment to Excellence, and all that!"

"Boy, you're crazy! What kind of job would the Raiders give you? 'Special Assistant in Charge of Dehydration'?"

"Huh?"

"I think your father means a water boy, Theodore," I said.

"Water boy? Hell no, I ain't gonna be no water boy!"

"What are you going to do, then? Let me hear a job description," Big Joe demanded.

"You ever heard of a trainer? I'm gonna be an assistant trainer! You know, one of those guys helps tape the fellas up before games, an' rubs 'em down after practice—stuff like that."

"Jeez Looweez," Big Joe said.

"I'm tellin' you, it's true. I swear it!"

"Boy, get off it. You aren't no assistant trainer. And anybody dumb enough to mistake you for one is too stupid to work for the Raiders."

"You don't understand. They're gonna *train* me, Pops. They're gonna *teach* me how to be a trainer."

"Who? Who's gonna teach you?"

"Cubby. Cubby Denkins. He's the head trainer for the Raiders, he's the one offered me the job."

"Cubby Denkins?" From the way Joe said the name, I could tell it was familiar to him. "Where would Cubby Denkins know you from?"

"I met him at this club, back in L.A. The Final Score. Him and a couple of the boys on the team came in one night last month, and we hit it off. You know, had a few drinks, talked a little 'ball. Next thing I know, he's offerin' me a job. An 'apprenticeship,' he called it. All I gotta do is pay for my materials, an' he'd do the rest, he said.''

"And these 'materials.' They're what you need a thousand dollars for?" I asked him.

"That's right."

"A *thousand dollars,* Theodore?"

"Yes ma'am." He was staring down into the Oreo bag, his head practically inside of it, ostensibly looking for a whole, unbroken cookie. I was going to ask him to look me in the eye and answer the question again, but his father spoke up before I got the chance.

"Hell, Dottie, what kind of 'materials' cost that kind of money? The team *bus* doesn't cost a thousand dollars!"

"It ain't *what* I gotta buy, Pops. It's *how much* I gotta buy. Like a hundred rolls of tape, three electronic stopwatches, twenty-five clipboards, two starter guns . . . It all adds up, man."

"So why do *you* have to buy it? Can't the Raiders supply you with all that crap?"

"Sure they could. 'Cept I'm not really gonna be workin' for the Raiders. Not at first, anyway. I'm gonna be workin' for Cubby. I'm gonna be his apprentice, like I told you."

"Yeah? So what?"

"So he's not gonna give me the job permanently— or pay any of my expenses—till he's satisfied I'm gonna work out. 'Cause the last apprentice he had, see, the guy ran out on him, an' took a ton of stuff with 'im when he left. Cubby had to reimburse the team out of his own pocket.''

Big Joe just looked at me and shook his head, not buying a word of Dog's story.

''What does all this have to do with Pittsburgh?'' I asked our son.

''That's where the Raiders are, Pittsburgh. They're playin' the Steelers there this Sunday.''

''And this couldn't have waited until they got back home?''

''No ma'am. It couldn't. After Pittsburgh, they go to Cleveland, and Cubby said he needs somebody right away. He wanted me to join the team 'fore they left L.A., but I didn't have the money then.''

''And you still don't,'' his father said flatly.

''What about the gun, Theodore? What are you doing with a gun?''

''Well, it's like this, Moms. I didn't really know it was a gun when I bought it. You know what I'm sayin'?''

''No,'' I said.

''Hell no,'' Big Joe said.

''Well, I needed a couple of starter guns, remember? You know, the kind of gun they use to start races at track meets? So I tried to buy one. On the street. Only, the lyin' chump I bought it from—''

''Sold you a real gun instead,'' I said.

Bad Dog nodded and blushed, embarrassed by his alleged naïveté.

''Okay. I've heard enough,'' Big Joe said to me. ''How about you? You heard enough?''

"Joe—"

"I say we buy him a ticket on the next Greyhound to California and let it go at that. What do you say?"

"I say we should give the boy a chance to prove his story before we do anything rash," I said.

"You want me to give him a chance? Fine. Here's what we'll do." Before I could stop him, he pushed past me to snatch Dog up off the floor by the nape of his neck. "I'm going to write a check for a thousand dollars and throw the both of 'em into the Canyon out there. If Junior hits the bottom before the check does, he can *have* it. Is that fair?"

"Joe, let the child go," I said quietly.

"Moms! He's not playin'!" Bad Dog gurgled, forced up on his tippytoes by the huge, ironlike hand around his throat.

"Joe, that's enough," I said. "You're scaring him."

Joe turned, keeping his grip on Dog, and said, "He's crazy, Dottie. A lunatic. We've been talking to him now for a whole day, and he hasn't made a lick of sense yet!"

"Of course he hasn't. This one never does. This is our baby, Joe. Theodore. Remember Theodore?"

He couldn't help but remember, eventually. Over the years, he and I had come to attach a specific profile to each of our five children, and we both knew them all by heart: Edward had always been the paranoid one, Delila the most impulsive; Walter was insensitive, and Mo was smart.

And Theodore, God bless him, was *slow*.

Only Snow White ever shared a home with a more

diverse band of little numbskulls.

"Besides," I went on, "we *all* have to stay at the park until they tell us otherwise. You know that."

"But, Dottie—"

"Baby, it's only for a few days, all right? Not even a week. We can stand to be around the boy for that long, can't we?"

Big Joe looked at his son and considered the question. It was like asking a Shiite Muslim if it wouldn't be too much trouble to share his toothbrush with a Christian for a day or two.

But he let Bad Dog go.

At last. A "baby" that worked.

_____ 3 __

Early the next morning, Big Joe and I went for our daily run, moving it up by several hours from the day before in the hope that an earlier starting time might change our luck a little, and this time, I checked to see that the door to our hotel cabin had locked behind us. Joe made a point of watching me do it, just as I thought he would, and mumbled something about the horse having already left the barn. I wanted to slap him silly, but I didn't; I knew I had his mistrust coming. After all, if I'd only locked Lucille's door the afternoon before . . .

Bad Dog wanted to stay in the room and sleep in until our return, but his father wouldn't have it.

"Get the hell out of that bed and go find something to do," Joe told him.

"Why? Why can't I just stay here?" Dog whined.

Joe crossed his arms and puffed up his chest. "Number one, because I don't want to find any more dead folks using my bathroom. And number two, because I said so. That's why."

"Man, that's cold."

"No it's not. Telling you to get out and stay out, that would be cold. Or begging you to get out of my life and never come back, *that* would be cold. Or asking you to leave this room—''

''All right, all right. I get the idea.'' Bad Dog rolled reluctantly out of bed and onto his feet, yawning. He reached down into the waistband of his shorts to scratch himself absently, looking me straight in the eye, then smiled and said, ''Mornin', Moms.''

My son, the gentleman's gentleman.

Outside, the sky was a perfect, milky blue at eight in the morning, marred only by a slow parade of cumulus clouds as white and wispy as stretched cotton balls. On the earth below, meanwhile, tourists of all nationalities streamed about the national park grounds like bees in a giant hive, either following the established trails or blazing new ones of their own, lugging infants and diaper bags, backpacks and lunch boxes—and cameras. Hundreds upon hundreds of cameras, all humming and clicking incessantly, and all focused upon a common target: the Grand Canyon. The great colossal void in the arid Arizona earth that stretched for miles in all directions, its jagged, burnt-orange walls carved and sculpted by time into cliffs and columns of every conceivable shape and size. Two hundred and seventeen miles long, the brochures said it was, and in some places as much as eighteen miles wide and 5,700 feet deep. It looked much larger than that.

We had been here three days now, and I still couldn't quite get over it. The colors, the lines, the seemingly limitless array of plateaus and precipices, all bathed in an ever shifting wash of sunlight and shadow—the place simply took my breath away.

As for Big Joe, I think he had seen enough that first day, when he learned that a party-size bag of Baconettes was going for almost four dollars at the only market/ liquor store on the park grounds.

"So what do you think?" he asked me a good ten minutes into our run along the Canyon's south rim, without any kind of lead-in to the question. "Now that you've had some time to sleep on it?"

"What do I think about what?"

"About what? About *him!* That brain surgeon son of yours. Who else?"

"Oh."

"You don't still think he's telling the truth, I know."

"You mean about the dead man yesterday?"

"I mean about everything. All that stuff about being offered a job with the Raiders, and needing a thousand dollars for clipboards and stopwatches—everything."

"Well . . ."

"Aw, Jeez Looweez, Dottie. Who the hell would hire that boy to be an assistant trainer? Only thing he knows about giving somebody a rubdown is how to use baby oil to put a Laker Girl in the mood."

"Yes, but . . ."

"But what?"

"But the boy's not a murderer, Joe. He might be a lot of things—"

"Like a liar."

"Yes."

"And a womanizer."

"Yes. That too. But—"

"And a perpetually unemployed sociopath who takes

advantage of his parents' kindness whenever the mood strikes him.''

"Yes, yes, of course. Theodore is all of those things, it's true. But a murderer?'' I shook my head. ''No. Not Theodore.''

"Okay. So he's not a murderer,'' Joe conceded. ''I'll grant you that. But he for damn sure knows more than he's been telling. I'd bet money on that. There's no way it's just a coincidence, him turning up inside Lucille at the same time as a corpse. No way. Tragedy doesn't strike the same family like that, one right after the other.''

That was basically how I felt about it too, but Big Joe didn't need to know that.

"All right,'' I said. ''So maybe he hasn't told us everything he knows. But he will, given time. Once his conscience starts to bother him a little. Don't you think?''

My husband looked over at me like I'd finally lost the last marble in my head. It was his way of reminding me that, while it was true I could always manage to squeeze the truth about something out of our son eventually, more often than not, I had to tear a switch from a tree first. Our front yard's constant state of defoliation was perfect testament to this fact.

"Okay,'' I said, ''so we have to make him talk.''

"Yes.''

"And we do that by . . . ?''

"By threatening to turn his behind in. That's how we do it. We go back there and tell him if he doesn't come clean, we're gonna call Crowe and Bollinger and tell

'em about the gun the boy had on him yesterday, like
we should have done in the first place.''

I shook my head. "He knows we'd never do that."

"You mean, he knows *you'd* never do that," Joe said.

I stopped running. Big Joe continued on for a few
yards, acting like he hadn't missed me, then turned
around and rejoined me, his legs still pumping away as
he jogged in place.

"Baby, that isn't funny. Those detectives find out
Theodore had a gun, you know what they'll do. They'll
take the boy in. Bullets or no bullets."

"And get the truth out of him in fifteen minutes,"
Big Joe said.

"Maybe. Maybe not. Either way, I think you and I
had better hear what the truth is before the law does.
Don't you?"

There wasn't a whole lot he could say to that. I'd
made too much sense.

"We're talking about a murder here, Dottie. Not a
jaywalking ticket," Big Joe said.

"I understand that."

He was surprised to learn that that was all I was going
to say. I'd already told him what I thought we should
do, and I wasn't going to sell him on the idea by arguing
with him. Not when a wifely stare-down could do the
job equally well, and without all the emotional muss and
fuss.

"Twenty-four hours," Big Joe said flatly, daring me
to reject the offer. "We'll give him just twenty-four
hours to 'fess up. He hasn't changed his tune by then,
told us why he's really here and how that dead man

ended up at our doorstep, we tell Crowe and Bollinger about the gun. No ifs, ands, or buts. Understand?''

I nodded my head and tried to look brave. "I understand," I said.

And with that, we ran the rest of our three miles in silence, at least one of us praying for the soul of our youngest son every inch of the way.

"Okay, now. Say cheese," Bad Dog said.

He was squinting through the viewfinder of a 35-mm camera, preparing to take the photograph of two blond, teenage girls standing before the curio-shop-in-pueblo's-clothing known as Hopi House. As Joe and I watched, Dog pressed the shutter button, then exchanged the camera with the shorter of the two girls for four quarters, accepting their lavish thanks with shamefully bogus humility. The hand-lettered sign he retrieved from the ground at his feet afterward read:

YOUR PICTURE TAKEN WITH YOUR CAMERA!
ONLY $1.00 PER SHOT
GET THE HOLE FAMILY IN THE PICTURE!
GUARANTEED PROFESSIONAL RESULTS!

"What the hell are you doing?" Big Joe asked him, his face reddening with embarrassment. "You want to get us all thrown out of here?"

"What? You told me to go out and find somethin' to do!"

"You know what I meant! A dollar to take somebody's photograph. Boy, that's highway robbery!"

"No it isn't. It's free enterprise."

"It's *bush*. That's what it is. You're taking advantage of these people, plain and simple. And you left the *w* out of 'whole'!"

Bad Dog glanced at his sign to see that his father was right, then started to defend himself further, only to find my hand clamped firmly across his mouth. "Your father's right, Theodore. You should be ashamed of yourself."

His jaw went slack, his eyes fell, and he nodded, duly ashamed.

"But tell me something. Just for the record. What's your take so far?"

"Thirty-seven bucks," Bad Dog said.

"In forty-five minutes?"

"Yes ma'am."

"Gimme that sign," I said.

Big Joe wheeled around, and Dog and I both broke up.

You want 'em to stick around awhile, girls, you've got to keep 'em on their toes.

I didn't have any money, but I went shopping anyway. We women can do that.

I hate to say it, but it's an art form that simply escapes most men. That's why they almost always refuse to come along. Joe says going shopping without money is like going fishing without a pole. You can watch all the fish swim by you want, but you can't take a single one home.

He doesn't get it.

Women like to shop because it's fun, not because it's profitable. As they say in the romance game, the chase is the thing, not the catch. Inspecting the goods, feeling an object's texture and weight, assessing its value compared to its price—it all makes for a very sensual experience. Finding a bargain you can blow some of your money on is just a bonus.

I told Joe and Bad Dog to entertain themselves for a while, then went straight to Hopi House, empty purse and all.

Hopi House is a wonderful little gift shop at the Grand Canyon's south rim—next to the El Tovar Hotel— which was modeled after the pueblos of the Native American village of the same name. The shop specializes in genuine Native American arts and crafts, primarily those of the Hopi and Navajo, and I had never seen more beautiful items in my life. Jewelry, pottery, woven rugs, and wood carvings—the color and craftsmanship of everything was simply exquisite. I had a field day.

Despite the fact that I couldn't shake the feeling I was being watched the whole time.

I'd round a corner, or be talking to a salesperson, and suddenly sense someone's eyes upon me. But when I'd turn to look—there'd be no one there. No one who showed the slightest interest in me, anyway.

It was odd, to say the least.

The last time it happened, I was stepping out a side door to leave. Again the feeling came over me that someone, somewhere behind me, was shadowing my every move. Ranger Cooper, or one of his brethren, I thought to myself, immediately resenting the idea. I was going to turn around one more time to look—and then I thought better of it, and stepped through the door and out of the building instead.

I stood just outside the door and waited to see who would be the next one through.

It was a clever plan, but it fell flat on its face when the door opened and a mass of humanity poured out. Or six people, to be more exact: two male/female couples and two individuals, a man and a woman, all grouped together like kids during a school fire drill. I couldn't make out the pairings until they split off in different directions, but by that time, I'd lost any chance I might have had to see if either of the two individuals had been surprised to find me standing there. I didn't think the woman had, but I wasn't so sure about the man. All I'd noticed about him was that he had a pair of binoculars hanging from his neck.

And now he was gone.

Less than a minute later, so was I.

"His name was Geoffry Bettis," Ranger Cooper said. "Geoffry Lamar Bettis. That name mean anything to any of you?"

One by one, we all shook our heads for his benefit. First Big Joe, then Bad Dog, then me. We were in his office at the ranger station in the village, sitting in various chairs around his desk. We were all a little nervous, but I was even more than that, as I had the additional pressure of having to keep my eyes off Cooper's face in general, and his mustache in particular. Big Joe was watching me like a hawk.

"He was a shoe salesman from Flagstaff," Cooper went on. "Forty-six years of age, married, with a couple of kids, both grown. No criminal arrest record, no outstanding warrants. Wife reported him missing two days ago—that's how we ID'd him." He looked up from the little notebook in his hand to face us again. "None of this sounds familiar to anybody?"

Once more, he watched as three heads swiveled from east to west. Nothing about the expression on Bad Dog's face gave me reason to believe the ranger's questions were making him particularly uncomfortable.

Cooper sipped a cup of coffee, pausing, I thought, to mull over his next move, and then consulted his notebook again. "His wife says he should have been driving a late-model Chevy subcompact, license number DMK four-two-six, but so far we haven't found it. Of course, he could have entered the park in a rented car or on a bus, or merely as a passenger in someone else's vehicle, but if he did, that's been difficult to prove. Just as it's been difficult to prove when, exactly, he arrived here. We're working on the assumption he got here yesterday, the same day he died, because we've found nothing to indicate he spent Monday night here—we've checked with all the hotels, and every guest is accounted for. Again, that doesn't rule out the possibility that he slept overnight inside a rental car, or inside somebody's motor home, et cetera, et cetera, but . . ." He shrugged and shook his head. "For now, we don't think so."

He finally closed the little notebook for good and looked up again, openly surveying our faces.

Suddenly, his mustache didn't look so adorable to me anymore.

"Folks, I'll be frank with you," he said. "I have no business calling you in here. This case belongs to the boys in the Sheriff's Department now, it's out of my hands. But since they've been kind enough to keep me abreast of how their investigation's going, I thought it would only be fair of me to do the same for you."

He paused, presumably waiting for one of us to thank him. We just let him wait.

"You see, it's like this. They don't think Mr. Bettis came all the way out here just to see the Canyon. The man had lived in Flagstaff for over twenty years—he and the family probably saw all of this place they could stand to see a decade ago."

"So he came out here to meet somebody," Big Joe said.

Cooper turned, impressed, and nodded his head. "Yessir, Mr. Loudermilk. That's their guess."

"And they think that somebody is one of us."

"I didn't say that, sir."

"But that *is* what they're thinking, isn't it?"

The ranger thought carefully about his answer, then said, "Let's just say, sir, that they find themselves wondering why Bettis died in your trailer, using your facilities, when he had so many other options available to him. Why break into a stranger's trailer to use the can—" He glanced at me, blushing, and said, " 'Scuse me, Mrs. Loudermilk. I meant to say the bathroom, of course." He turned to Joe again. "Why break into a stranger's trailer to use the *bathroom* when there are public rest rooms all over the park?"

"Maybe he couldn't find a public rest room," I suggested.

"Or maybe he couldn't wait to find one," Big Joe added.

"Hey. When you gotta go, you gotta go," Bad Dog said, throwing in his two cents.

Cooper gave our son a disapproving look, momentarily forgetting Dog's father and me altogether. "Maybe," he said, without a trace of warmth in his voice.

"I mean, man, I can remember more than a few times when I couldn't find a public head, and I had to—"

"You been traveling with your parents long?" Cooper asked abruptly, cutting Dog off.

"What?"

"I asked if you've been traveling with your folks here long. The three of you have been together, what—a few days? A few weeks? What?"

Dog stole a pitifully conspicuous glance at me, all but admitting that he had forgotten how the three of us had agreed to answer Cooper's question if it happened to come up.

"Come on, son," Cooper snapped. "I'm asking you a simple question. You don't really need your mother's help to answer it, do you?"

"He's been with us for three weeks," Joe said, surprising all of us.

"Pardon me, Mr. Loudermilk, but I'm talking to the boy here."

"The 'boy' here is twenty-two years old, officer. And he's my son. Which means as long as I'm in the room to hear it, you're gonna show him some respect when you talk to him. You got that?"

"I was merely—"

"You were merely talking to him like a four-year-old you'd caught taking cookies from a jar," I said, backing my husband up. "Theodore is a man. If you treat him like one, he'll tell you anything you want to know. Won't you, Theodore?"

Dog was still staring at his father, thrilled to the core by Joe's unsolicited rush to his defense.

"I said, won't you, Theodore?"

He turned. "Huh? Oh, yes ma'am!" He nodded energetically for Cooper's benefit. "Anything you want to know."

"Look," Big Joe said. "He's just as confused about all of this as we are. All right? What we all told you yesterday still stands. We didn't know this man Bettis, and we sure as hell didn't invite him into our trailer to use the bathroom. He invited himself in, while we were out. Why, we don't know. I'm sorry."

"Then none of you had any plans to meet with Bettis before he was murdered."

"No. How could we? *We didn't know the man.*"

"I see," Cooper said, though he quite clearly didn't.

"Look," Bad Dog said. "I don't get it. This Bettis guy's wallet was missing, right? And all his cash?"

Cooper nodded solemnly.

"So what's the mystery? The man was robbed. Somebody probably entered my parents' trailer through the open door, just like he did, and held him up at gun-point. Cleaned him out, then shot him dead.''

''Why?''

''Why what?

''Why shoot him dead? Why shoot him at all? He was sitting on the toilet with his pants around his ankles, for crying out loud. Why would the thief need to shoot him?''

Bad Dog thought about it for a moment, then said, ''That's a good question.''

Big Joe lowered his head and shook it from side to side, the way fathers with little patience for thickheaded sons so often do.

''Maybe he gave the thief an argument,'' I said, trying to come to Dog's rescue. ''I know I certainly would have, if someone had burst in on me while I was . . . while I was . . .''

''Indisposed,'' Cooper offered.

''Yes. Indisposed. I mean, that's such an *inopportune* time to rob someone, don't you think? I would have been very upset if someone had done that to me, when they could have just as easily waited until my business was through to conduct theirs. If you know what I mean.''

I suspected what I'd just said had sounded foolish, but I wasn't really sure until I found my husband shaking his head at the floor again, a little more emphatically this time.

Generously ignoring Joe's wordless editorializing, Ranger Cooper smiled at me and said, ''You make a good point, ma'am. Mr. Bettis may have put up a fight, at that.'' He shrugged. ''However, I should point out that if he did, it would have had to be a very short one.''

''Why is that?''

''Because there were no signs of a struggle in the bathroom,'' Joe said.

''I didn't say he put up a fight, Ranger Cooper,'' I said, turning to our host again. ''I said, perhaps he gave his killer an *argument.* In other words—''

''It was something he said that got him killed, rather than something he did.''

''Yes.''

After a while, Cooper nodded. ''I suppose that's certainly possible, yes, ma'am. If he was killed by someone who was already highly aggravated, for example, it could have easily been a wrong word here or there that got him shot.'' He turned to face Big Joe. ''Wouldn't you say so, Mr. Loudermilk?''

Joe didn't like the sound of the question, and neither did I. ''That all depends on what you mean by 'highly aggravated,' '' Big Joe said.

''I mean angry. Upset. The way someone might be if they thought they'd just caught a stranger in the act of burglarizing their home, for example.''

Big Joe just sat there, doing a slow burn.

''You wouldn't happen to own any firearms yourself, would you, sir?'' Cooper asked him, pressing his luck.

''I'm afraid not,'' my husband said.

''Really? You mean an ex-lawman like yourself doesn't keep a little protection of some sort close at hand, just in case?''

''No. I don't.''

"I take it they haven't found the murder weapon yet," I said, trying to steer Cooper away from the fight he seemed determined to lure Big Joe into.

"No ma'am. As a matter of fact, I regret to say they haven't."

"Well, lookee here," Big Joe said, jumping right back into the fray. "You're not going to find it by hassling us. I can promise you that. But you wanna pat us all down to see for yourself, rather than just take my word for it, come on. All right? Come on ahead, you can start with *me* . . ."

"Now, Joe—" I said, sensing a bad scene coming on.

"No. No! The man obviously isn't satisfied that the three of us are all just innocent bystanders in this whole mess, so I say, let him do whatever he has to do to *become* satisfied. We've got nothing to hide, right?"

"Mr. Loudermilk, I think you're overreacting," Cooper said mildly.

"Overreacting? I beg to differ with you, officer. When Joe Loudermilk overreacts, heads roll and molars fly. You understand what I'm saying?"

"Pops, take it easy," Bad Dog implored his father.

"Take it easy, nothing! He's accusing me of murder!"

"I didn't accuse anyone of anything," the ranger said. "I merely suggested—"

"That I mistook Bettis for a burglar and put a bullet in his chest."

"He *was* in your home uninvited, was he not? Isn't

that what you've been telling us all along?''

"Yes, but—''

"So what else would you have taken him for but a
burglar? If he had come into your trailer while all of you
were out, like you say, it could have only been for one
reason: to burglarize the place. Not just to use the bathroom. He could have done that as an afterthought.''

"Except that he was already dead when we found
him,'' I said.

"Yes,'' Cooper said, turning. "So you say.''

"So I *say?* You mean, so it *is!* We don't have to lie
to you, Ranger Cooper. And you don't have to follow
us around all over this park just to be sure of that. We're
not hiding anything. From you, or anyone else.''

"Excuse me, Mrs. Loudermilk, but nobody's been
following you people anywhere. Nobody from *my* office,
anyway.''

"I don't care whose office they're from. I don't like
being spied upon, and I want it to stop.''

"But—''

"Look,'' Big Joe said, demanding the ranger's attention again. "If we'd killed that white man for the reasons
you're suggesting, we would've told you so, all right?
We'd have caught a little hell for shooting an unarmed
man, sure, but that would've been about it. Two fright-
ened *old* people protecting their home against an un-
known intruder, that's all it would've looked like to you.
Just an unfortunate episode, highly regrettable yet ultimately harmless. You would've let us all go without
filing charge one, I'll bet. Wouldn't you?''

Cooper didn't want to, but eventually he nodded his head. "I imagine that's how it would have worked out, yes."

"All right then. That means we had no reason to lie to you, doesn't it? Why lie when the truth can set you free?"

"Amen," Bad Dog said.

Big Joe turned to glower at him.

"Sorry," Bad Dog said.

"What you say makes sense to me," Ranger Cooper said, admitting the fact with as much grace as he could muster, "but those Sheriff's Department boys, they're a sight more skeptical about these things than I am. They like to think everybody's lying, all the time. Me, on the other hand, I believe most people will tell you the truth the very first time they're asked for it. Or at least the *second* time they're asked, anyway."

He was looking at me expectantly, thinking he could charm me into making some kind of confession. When I failed to offer him one, he sighed and said, "Well, I've imposed on you people enough for one day, huh? Thank you all for coming in, and enjoy the rest of your stay at the park."

He smiled, and his mustache did its sexy little dance, but this time I didn't feel much of anything for it.

In fact, the nasty little fur ball just made me nauseous.

"Dynamite stone guard. What'd that hit you for?"

"Two-ten. I got a great deal on it."

"Had any trouble with your door gaskets? I've always

heard the door gaskets on Sovereigns need constant replacement.''

"Not mine. I had a guy I know back home in St. Cloud treat my gaskets—windows, doors, everything—and I've only had to replace 'em once.''

"St. Cloud? You're from St. Cloud?''

"That's right.''

"Then you've gotta know Artie Dobbins. He's WBCCI out of St. Cloud.''

"Sure, I know Artie. Met him at the International back in '91. We lived less than twenty miles from each other, and never even knew it until then. He's a funny guy, Artie, isn't he?''

Big Joe and Albert Gunderson began to laugh, just thinking about how funny a guy Artie Dobbins was.

We had just made Albert's acquaintance ten minutes ago, as we were walking through the trailer park we had spent Monday night in, feeling more at home here than at the hotel. It's a difficult thing to explain to laymen, but once a person becomes a full-timer—someone who, like Joe and myself, lives year-round on the road—he can't take the sensation of solid ground beneath his feet for very long. For just as a sailor eventually learns to move with the rhythm of the sea, full-timers have learned to walk in accordance with the quirky bounce of a trailer's suspension, a soft, often noisy motion the earth simply cannot duplicate.

Our Lucille had been gone now for less than eight hours, but already withdrawal from this sensation was making a nervous wreck out of Joe. I knew when he suggested the diversion to the trailer park that he would find another Airstream within fifteen minutes of our arrival, and that he would get himself invited inside of it only seconds after that.

Enter Albert Gunderson of St. Cloud, Minnesota, and his gorgeous little twenty-one-foot Sovereign. Joe had pounced on him as he was making a careful inspection of his butane tanks, and immediately struck up a conversation. Once Joe had established our credentials as members in good standing of the Wally Byam Caravan Club International, Region 12, Albert took us to his bosom like a shepherd embracing his sheep. For invoking the name of Wally Byam—the late, great founder of the Airstream empire—is a sure-fire way to make any Airstream owner a friend of yours for life.

"So you and Artie made the International in '91, huh?" Joe asked Albert, obviously envious.

The small man with the skittish toupee nodded proudly. "Sure did. Didn't you?"

"Wish I could say I did, but no, I'm afraid I didn't. The wife and I didn't come aboard until just last year. But we were up in Dayton."

"Dayton was a blast!"

"Tell me about it!"

"You've gotta see this beer mug I bought in Dayton. It'll crack you up!"

Albert started for the door to his trailer and gestured for us all to follow.

"*I'm* not goin' in there," Bad Dog said to me, under his breath so his father wouldn't hear. He and I had been standing together off to the side, listening to Joe and his new best pal chatter without really hearing a single word.

"Come on," Big Joe called to us, waiting to see what we were going to do.

"You go on ahead," I told him. "We're just going to wait out here and talk."

Joe wasn't sure he liked the sound of that, but he was sharp enough to see that I didn't care to elaborate, so he simply entered the trailer after Albert and let us be.

"I think you need to get Pops to a doctor, Moms," Bad Dog said moments later. "He's takin' this 'King of the Road' business way too seriously."

"Theodore—"

"But he was somethin' else back at the ranger's office, wasn't he? The way he stood up for me like that, I mean?"

"Your father loves you, Theodore. Very much."

"Hey, and I love him. It's just that, I don't know, sometimes—"

"Listen. We're not out here to talk about your father."

"We're not?"

"No."

"Then we must be out here to talk about my money. Right?"

"Among other things. Yes."

A grin slid snakelike across his face, putting every tooth in his mouth on display. "You're gonna give it to me, aren't you? Man, I knew it! I knew I could count on Moms!"

"You mean, you *thought* you could count on Moms.

Moms isn't having any of your nonsense this time, Theodore. This time, you've gone too far.''

''What? What'd I do now?''

''You know perfectly well what you've done. You've mixed your own parents up in murder, that's what, and you don't even have the decency to tell us *why!*''

''Me?''

''Your father and I have been lying through our teeth to protect you up to now, young man, but no more. You understand? I want the truth, and I want it now. Every single word of it.''

''The truth?''

Again, the overwhelming power I held over my son was beginning to work its magic. His eyes were expanding with fear and his lips started to tremble as the dreadful realization that he was about to tell me everything I wanted to know slowly hit him.

''Moms—'' he started to say, before all hell broke loose in the park behind us.

''Lemme go! Lemme go before I hurt somebody!'' we heard a booming voice cry, in the midst of what sounded like a small riot breaking out. We turned around to find a handful of park rangers falling all over themselves trying to subdue a gigantic black man, less than thirty yards from where we were standing. They had managed to get a pair of handcuffs on him and were now trying to shoehorn him into the back seat of a patrol car, but they would have probably had an easier time wrestling with a live rhinoceros. The big man wasn't budging.

''I was just askin' the man a coupla questions!'' he growled, standing his ground against the wall of uniformed bodies pressing against him. "What's wrong with that?"

He was the biggest human being I had ever seen. His chest was as wide as a small Toyota, and his thighs were as thick as oil barrels. He had a diminutive waist, no neck to speak of, and was wearing a pair of wraparound sunglasses that made his bull-like countenance even more imposing than it already was.

"Hey! Isn't that—?" Big Joe started to ask, suddenly standing right beside me.

"Come on, pal! Get in the goddamn car!" one of the exhausted rangers pleaded, before Joe could finish his question.

"We just want to ask you a few questions! Take it easy!" another ranger promised the big man, even shorter of breath than his friend.

As a growing crowd of people gathering in the trailer park watched in awe, the giant held firm for a solid minute more, unshaken and unbowed, then simply shrugged his massive shoulders and said, "Okay, okay! I got nothin' to hide. Let's go."

And with that, he lowered himself into the back of the patrol car with the greatest of ease, like a little boy going for a Sunday drive with the family. Visibly relieved, and amazed by their sudden good fortune, the rangers slammed the door on him quickly, before he could change his mind, then piled into their respective patrol cars and escorted him away, leaving all of us at the trailer park to speculate wildly about what we had just seen, and what it could have possibly meant.

"You said you knew who that was?" I asked, turning

to Big Joe. He seemed to be in a daze.

"I don't know. It looked like . . . " He let his voice trail off.

"Who?"

"But hell, that doesn't make any sense. He wouldn't have no business bein' out here."

"Who?"

"Dozer Meadows. Left defensive end for the Raiders. Four-time All-Pro, the best in the business."

"The *Raiders?*"

"Yeah." He turned around himself to get Bad Dog's opinion. "Wasn't that—?"

But Bad Dog, who'd been standing in our shadows only seconds ago, wasn't there anymore.

Somehow, I wasn't terribly surprised.

4

Ever hear the expression "A day late, and a dollar shy"?

That's the story of my children, right there. Oh so close to being good kids, yet not quite there. They're always just missing, coming within inches of doing the right thing before drifting off to do the wrong one. They fail by the merest fractions of time, space, and cabfare.

Even Mo.

She isn't as bad as the others, no, but she has her moments.

"Now, Mom, don't get excited, but I think I should warn you about something," she said as soon as I picked up the phone. It was as if she were calling me of her own accord, and not in response to the message I had left on her answering machine an hour ago, telling her where her father and I could be reached.

"We know," I said.

"Bad Dog was by my place a few weeks ago, and I think he went through my mail. I'm not sure, but I think he knows where you guys are, and intends to go out there looking for you."

"We know," I said again.

"You know? What do you mean, you know?"

"I mean, your brother's been with us now for almost two days. But thanks for the warning, just the same. It's good to know there's always someone there to alert your father and me to life-threatening disasters that happened to us over forty-eight hours ago, just in case we failed to notice on our own."

"He's already there?"

"Yes, Mo. He's already here. He slipped you a curve and *flew* to Arizona, rather than walk the whole way."

"All right, Mother," my daughter said, no doubt sensing a well-deserved guilt complex coming on. "I'm sorry. I should have called you and Daddy earlier, obviously."

"Don't be silly. You only had two weeks."

"Listen. Are you going to be civil, or do I have to ask you to put my father on the phone?"

"Go ahead. See how much good it'll do you."

We both laughed. We do a lot of that, Mo and I.

"So tell me," she said. "What's he up to this time? Or do I want to know?"

I told her everything, from my discovery of Bad Dog in our closet to the scene involving Dozer Meadows at the trailer park less than two hours ago. Naturally, she interrupted me every thirty seconds or so to ask if I was joking, but overall she took the news rather well. Her initial comment aside, anyway.

"Let me kill him, Mom. Please. I'm a lawyer, I know how to get away with these things."

"You're being judgmental, Mo," I said.

"Mother, he's involved you two in a *homicide* this

time! That's just a tad more serious than petty larceny, you know.''

"Now, Mo, we all agreed we weren't going to talk about that incident anymore, didn't we? Theodore told us he didn't know those encyclopedias were written in Spanish, and the judge believed him.''

"The judge threw the case out of court for lack of evidence, Mother. Not because he thought Dog was innocent.''

"All the same. Your father and I are not completely convinced he had anything to do with that dead man. He just turned up at an awkward time, that's all.''

Mo made a sound conveying one part amusement, three parts disgust, but she didn't pursue her argument any further. She just said, ''I think maybe I'd better come down there.''

"No, no, no. Absolutely not.''

I could see her and Big Joe now, drawing lots to see who would get Dog's clothes after the crucifixion.

"Why not?''

"Because it isn't necessary. Your father and I can handle this ourselves.''

"Really? How?''

"By giving him one more chance to tell us the truth. And I mean every word of it, this time.''

Sitting on the bed nearby in our hotel cabin, his father towering over him like the sword of Damocles, Bad Dog heard this and turned to face me, sweating king-size bullets.

"And if he doesn't tell you the truth?'' Mo asked.

"We'll cross that bridge when we come to it," I said.

She didn't much care for that answer, of course, but I guess I'd worn her down to the point where she lacked the strength to press the issue. She just sighed with heavy heart and asked me for the name and number of the investigating officer who was handling our case for the Sheriff's Department, saying she intended to call him as soon as we were through, just to see how things were going.

"Be polite to the man, Mo," I told her, after I'd given her the information she wanted.

"Yes, Mother."

"None of that 'Touch my parents and I'll sue you into the next Ice Age' business, like you pulled at Lake Tahoe. You hear?"

"I hear you, Mother."

"Dottie, leave the child alone," Big Joe said.

"We can't go back to Harrah's now, did you know that? We used to stay there all the time, did almost all of our gambling there, but not anymore. We can't show our faces at the door at Harrah's now. They hear the name Loudermilk and boom!—everyone turns cold as ice."

"Mom, they were trying to cheat you."

"Out of three dollars and seventeen cents."

"A payoff is a payoff, Mother."

"It was a penny slot machine, Mo."

"Get off the phone, Dottie," Big Joe said.

Having ignored him once already, I decided to feign obedience and did as I was told.

• • •

"All right, Theodore. Let's have it."

"Have what?"

"Joe, go get me my strap."

"Strap? What d'you want with a strap?" Bad Dog started to laugh nervously. "Hell, you can't whip me! I'm twenty-two years old, I'm a grown man!"

"I don't care how old you are. Long as I'm breathing, any child of mine asking for a good spanking is going to get one. Guaranteed."

"Moms, you're not going to whip me. All right?"

"And just how do you think you're going to stop me? With your father right here in the same room?"

He stopped laughing. He hadn't thought about his father, and his silence proved it. If he so much as raised a hand against me, Joe would make him wish he'd taken his whipping, and liked it. Twenty-two or no twenty-two.

Big Joe turned away from the closet to hand me a wide, black leather belt with a heavy silver buckle. Like me, he was as stone-faced as an undertaker at his own funeral.

"Want me to hold him down for you?"

"All right, hold it, hold it, hold it!" Bad Dog said, showing his father and me the palms of both hands in an effort to hold us at bay. "I get the idea, all right? You want the truth. All of it."

Neither Big Joe nor I said a word. In fact, we didn't move, save for my coiling and uncoiling the black belt around one hand, slowly and methodically, over and over again.

"Okay. Okay. What do you want to hear first?"

"Let's start with this person Dozer Meadows," I said.

"Sure. What about him?"

"You tell us," Big Joe said. "You're the one who took off like a scared rabbit when he showed up at the trailer park this afternoon. Why was that?"

"Took off like a scared rabbit? Me? No way, man. I just went for a walk, that's all."

"Theodore," I said, "you were hiding in the closet again. Remember? We just pulled you out of there twenty minutes ago!"

"Hey, I told you, Moms. I was lookin' for a quarter. I dropped some change on the floor, and a quarter rolled into the closet under the door. So I went in there to get it. All right?"

Big Joe turned to me and said, "As I was saying. Would you like me to hold him down for you, or not?"

"Okay, okay! I was hidin' in there, yeah! I was in the closet *hidin'!*"

"From Dozer Meadows," I said.

"Yeah, that's right. From Dozer Meadows."

"Why? What's he got to do with you?"

"Nothin'. 'Cept that he wants to *kill* me."

"Kill you? For what?"

"For gettin' him suspended from the team. What else?"

"You mean suspended from the Raiders?"

"Of course I mean the Raiders! Who else would I be talkin' about, the *Mighty Ducks?*"

"Oh, *Jeez Looweez,*" Joe moaned, apparently grasping our son's meaning much faster than I. "You trying to tell us that *you're* the reason that boy got booted off the team?'' The possibility had him near tears.

"Well, yes and no," Bad Dog said, "dependin' on how you look at it."

"Jeez Loooweeez," his father groaned again, stretching the last word out to magnify his distress.

"That's why I wanna go to Pittsburgh. To get him reinstated."

"Best player on the whole damn team! The one man that pitiful defense can least afford to lose!"

"You didn't hear what I said, Pops. I said, if you could just get me to Pittsburgh—"

"Will somebody please tell me what in the world you two are talking about?" I cried, feeling the tide of Bad Dog's interrogation rolling completely out of my reach. "Dozer Meadows was suspended from the team—all right, that much I understand. Which means he can't play ball, at least for a while, right?"

"Right," Dog said.

"For how long?"

"Two weeks."

"Says who?"

"Says the coach. Terry Bell."

"All right. Why?"

"For conduct detrimental to the team," Joe said angrily. "For partying so extensively the night before last Sunday's game, he was only good for seven sorry minutes in the game itself."

"He made a key tackle, though," Bad Dog said.

"He threw up on the guy," Big Joe said.

"It was a nine-yard loss."

"In a game we lost by twenty-four points. To the

Cincinnati Bengals. At *home!*''

"I take it the Cincinnati Bengals aren't very good," I said.

Joe looked at me and grimaced. "The Raiders were favored by twenty-one," he said.

"Hey. 'On any given Sunday . . .' " his son reminded him.

"So Dozer was suspended for two weeks," I said, trying to keep our conversation on track.

"Yeah. And fined a thousand bucks. Strictly to save face, you know? Because the sports guys on TV, man, they must've shown the clip of him upchuckin' on Drew Archer's shoes about a million times that night. Over and over again, they ran it. Made you sick just to watch it."

"Did you say he was fined a thousand dollars?"

"Yeah. See, they—"

"A thousand dollars?" I asked again.

All of a sudden, Dog clammed up, finally realizing what he'd said.

"Uh-huh. You see there?" Big Joe asked me, starting to bounce around on the balls of his feet as his blood pressure began to rise to new heights. "What'd I tell you, Dottie? What'd I tell you? He wasn't up for any job with the Raiders! He wanted that money so he could pay Meadows's fine!"

"I *told* you—he's lookin' to *kill* me! I don't pay his fine and get him back on the team in time for the Steeler game this Sunday, he's gonna tear me apart!"

"Why, Theodore?" I demanded, anxious to get the truth out of him before his father felt compelled to try.

"Why does he blame *you* for his getting suspended?"

"Because he was out partyin' with *me* last Saturday night," he said, blurting the words out before he could stop himself. "When I was supposed to be . . . well . . ." He shrugged, the way he had as a five-year-old whenever we'd ask him *how he could do such a thing*. "When I was supposed to be *watching* him, like."

"Watching him? You mean following him?"

"No. I mean *watchin'* him. Baby-sittin' him. Goin' everywhere he goes, to keep him out of trouble, an' stuff."

"To keep him *out* of trouble? *You?*" Big Joe asked, incredulous.

"Yessir. Cubby said to hang with him all weekend and keep him away from booze, drugs, and women. 'Cause Dozer, man, he's got no self-control, right? He doesn't know when to quit."

Joe started laughing. Hard.

"Joe, get ahold of yourself," I told him. But I was smiling when I said it.

"It ain't funny, Pops," Bad Dog said sadly.

"No. It certainly is not," I agreed, just before losing it myself.

Bad Dog sat there and watched us, two old fools laughing and gasping for breath like drunks at a wine-tasting party.

"I'm sorry, baby," I said to him when I was finally able to speak again, "but you have to admit, it is pretty ridiculous. Somebody hiring you to keep somebody else out of trouble."

"Yeah? And why's that?"

'' 'Cause that's like hiring a rat to keep the mice out of the cheese,'' Big Joe said, wiping tears from his eyes. "That's why. Trouble's your middle name, boy!''

The look on Dog's face said he wanted desperately to dispute that, but he knew it couldn't be done. His checkered past spoke for itself.

"How did you get the job in the first place, Theodore?'' I asked him.

"I told you. Cubby gave it to me. We were always runnin' into each other at the Final Score, like I said, and every time we did, I'd bug him for a job on the team. Any kind of job, I said, I'll do anything you want, just ask.

"So one night he says, okay, maybe there *is* somethin' I can do. Somethin' that could lead to a permanent position as an assistant trainer, if I did the job right. So I said, what is it? and he said all I gotta do is hang with Dozer Meadows for half the weekend, Friday and Saturday night. Go where he goes, do what he does, and keep him from gettin' too crazy. You know, don't let him overindulge. Because—''

"Because he'd had a run-in with the police on a DUI earlier in the season,'' Big Joe said to me, not trusting our son to tell the story himself. "In Beverly Hills. He totaled a parked car making an illegal U-turn and banged himself up pretty good. You couldn't read about anything else in the sports pages for a week.''

"So the Raiders wanted somebody to watch him,'' I said to Bad Dog.

He nodded his unruly head. "Yeah. At least until they left for Pittsburgh, anyway. All they wanted to do was make sure he got through the Cincinnati game without killin' himself, Cubby said.''

"And Dozer went along with this?''

"Sure. He and I clicked up, we were homies. That's why Cubby picked me for the job. He'd seen us hangin' together at the club all the time, so he knew the Doze and me were tight.''

"The Doze?''

"That's what all his friends call him, yeah. The Doze.''

"And you're saying he didn't mind that you were going to be his baby-sitter. He didn't resent the fact in any way.''

"Naw. In fact, he actually thought it was a good idea, havin' somebody around him all the time to tell him when he was about to mess up. He appreciated it, even.''

"So what went wrong, then?'' Big Joe asked him.

Our son was suddenly struck stupid. Or at least, more stupid than usual. "Huh?''

"You heard what I said. What went wrong? How did he end up messing up anyway?''

"Oh.'' He wriggled around on the couch like he was trying to dislodge a live hamster from his trousers. "Well, I guess because I tried too hard. You know.''

"What do you mean, you tried too hard? You tried too hard *how?*''

"Well . . . by sort of outthinkin' myself, I guess.''

"Outthinking yourself?''·

"Yessir. See, the first night I watched him—Friday— I just followed around behind him. He did all the drivin', and I did all the ridin', and we ended up goin' to all his regular hangouts, all the places Cubby said he liked to get in trouble in.''

''And?''

''And, well, Cubby was right. The Doze almost messed up two, maybe three times that night. He kept threatenin' to run off with this homie, or that, or the young ladies at one table or another. You know.

''So the next night, Saturday, I figured, maybe I should change his pattern a little bit. Like, change his routine, keep him out of the places he likes to go, and away from all the people he likes to run with. Protect him from any bad influences, like.

''So what I did was, I made him hang with *me* Saturday night, 'stead of the other way around. You understand? I picked all the places we went that night, not him, and they were all places he'd never been to before, places where he didn't know a soul. I thought that would be the best thing for him.''

''But it wasn't,'' I said.

''No. It was the *worst* thing for him, the way it worked out. 'Cause around his friends, see, he was just one of the guys, right? But around strangers, he was . . . well, he was the *Doze!* The Man! Bigger than life, and all that. The brothers and sisters in all the places I took him to treated him like royalty, like he was a god from Mount Olympics, or somethin'.''

''Mount *Olympus*,'' Big Joe said dourly.

''Mount Olympus, right. Like in the Thor comic books.''

''Go on, Theodore,'' I said.

''Huh? Oh, yeah. Where was I?''

"They were treating him like royalty."

"Oh, yeah. Like royalty! Like they'd never seen a professional football player before, or somethin'. They were all over the man like white on rice, offerin' him this and that, buyin' him one drink after another. Seemed like every time I turned around, somebody was slippin' a business card into his hand, or askin' him to autograph a napkin. And the women! Pops, it was somethin' else. They wouldn't *stop* comin' over to our table! Offerin' the Doze their phone numbers, or bendin' over and pullin' the front of their dresses down so he could autograph their—"

"Never mind, Theodore," I said.

"Autograph their *what?*" Big Joe demanded.

"I said never mind," I told him.

He caught the fire in my eye and let the subject drop, but only after he and his son had exchanged a brief but purposeful nod, making a promise to each other I was not supposed to be sharp enough to pick up on: *We'll talk later.*

"So what you're saying is that you would have been better off going to all of his regular hangouts," I said to Bad Dog.

"Yes ma'am. Of course, he might've got just as jacked up goin' to his places as he did mine, but he probably wouldn't have done it so fast. 'Cause, see, you can get pretty wasted just payin' for *half* your drinks, but when you don't have to pay for *none* of 'em . . ."

"We get the picture," Big Joe said.

"What I don't understand is why you didn't intervene when you saw things getting out of hand," I said sternly.

"I didn't *see* things gettin' out of hand," Bad Dog replied, somewhat defensively.

"Why not? You were there, weren't you? You were watching him, weren't you?"

"Yes ma'am, I was watchin' him. But . . ."

"But what?"

"But I wasn't really *seein'* him. You know what I mean?"

"No. I don't." I turned to Big Joe. "Do you?"

My husband just looked at our son and said, "Tell your mother how many drinks *you* paid for that night, boy."

Of course, the answer was none.

"Lord, have mercy," I said.

"I hung with 'im for about three hours, then the lights went out," Bad Dog said. "By the time it occurred to me that maybe he was overdoin' it, man, I was too far gone to care. Last thing I remember, this brickhouse in a leather skirt was pullin' down the zipper on one side and askin' the Doze to write his phone number on her—"

"Don't you start that again," I said. "So you fell down on the job and let Dozer get smashed. The next day, he played a terrible game and got suspended from the team. Is that right?"

"Yes ma'am."

"And everyone blamed you for what happened."

"Yes."

"And that's why Dozer wants to kill you."

"Yes."

"Okay. So far, so good. That leaves us with only one

unanswered question, doesn't it?''

"What's that?''

"How in the hell did he find you?'' Big Joe asked, cutting in. "Way the hell out here at the Grand Canyon?''

Bad Dog bit his lip and tried not to meet my gaze directly, afraid to say another word.

"You didn't tell him you were coming here, did you?'' I asked, already certain that I knew the answer.

"Moms, I *had* to,'' Bad Dog said, his eyes pleading for forgiveness. "He was gonna destroy me! I had to say I was gonna do *something* to make things right for him again!''

"So you told him you were going to get his fine money from us. Is that what you're telling me?''

"And then square things away with him and Cubby, yeah.''

"Then he knows all about your father and me. And Lucille.''

"Lucille?''

"Our trailer home, Theodore,'' I said.

He shrugged. "Oh. Well . . . he doesn't know it by *name,* or anything, but—''

"Don't stop me this time, Dottie,'' Big Joe said abruptly, his face as red and luminous as a stoplight. "When I grab hold of the boy this time to break him in half, *please don't stop me!*''

I was tempted not to, but I did.

"Pops, I told you!'' Bad Dog cried. "I didn't have any choice! He asked me how I was gonna come up with that kind of money, and I told 'im the only thing

I could think of—that I was gonna come out here and get it from you. What else could I do?''

''You could've taken your lumps like a man and left your mother and me out of this whole mess. That's what you could've done!'' Joe started to pace anxiously about the room, his hands going this way and that as he ranted and raved. ''Took forty-seven park rangers to get that man in the back seat of a car, he rips the heads off quarterbacks like I pop the caps on catsup bottles, and who's he out here looking for, thanks to you? Us, that's who! Two old people who couldn't stop him from wringin' our necks if you gave us a ten-minute head start and an M-sixteen!''

''Pops, I didn't know he was gonna follow me! The plan was, he was supposed to wait in L.A. for me to come back with the money.''

''So why didn't he?''

''Well. I guess because . . .'' He didn't—or wouldn't—finish the thought.

''Because he didn't know that *was* the plan,'' Big Joe guessed.

''No sir. See, he kept insisting on comin' along, I couldn't talk 'im out of it! But I knew if I brought 'im with me, and you guys refused to give me the money, well . . . somebody was gonna get *hurt*.''

Joe stopped pacing. He pointed a giant finger at Bad Dog's face, glaring at him the way a Hatfield would glare at a McCoy, and said, ''Somebody's gonna get hurt, all right. You were damn sure right about that!''

''Joe,'' I said, ''take it easy now.''

''In fact, somebody's gonna get hurt right now, right

this minute, unless they get the hell out of my sight by the time I count to three! One, two—''

''Joe!''

Bad Dog didn't bother saying good-bye. I felt a rush of wind behind me, heard the screen door of our cabin slam shut, and he was gone.

Had Joe decided to chase after him, I would've been glad to let him go, but he didn't. He just stood where he was and waited for his anger to dissipate, checking his no doubt accelerated pulse rate as he did so.

''Joe,'' I said calmly, almost demurely. ''I wish you hadn't done that.''

He scowled at me, unrepentant. ''Yeah? Why?''

I smiled. ''Because we still don't know why someone left a dead white man in our bathroom yesterday. Do we?''

My husband's chin fell to his chest, and his head began to turn from side to side in a dance of pure despair. ''Aw—''

''I know, baby. *Jeez Looweez,*'' I said.

_____ 5 __

We had to hear him say "I don't know" a hundred times before we were sure, but later that afternoon Big Joe and I came to be convinced that Bad Dog really _didn't_ have the slightest idea why a corpse had turned up inside our trailer home on the same fateful day as he. His story was just too unwavering to be fake; Dog could always tell a lie well, but only if he didn't have to repeat it more than once or twice. Apparently, he'd discovered the late Geoffry Lamar Bettis in our bathroom just as he'd always insisted, and had never laid eyes on the poor man beforehand. Furthermore, it seemed, he had no idea what connection there could possibly be between Bettis and Dozer Meadows, short of the fact that Meadows had ostensibly come to the Grand Canyon hoping to commit a murder, and Bettis had already become the victim of one. We asked Dog if he thought his friend "the Doze" was deranged enough to have killed an innocent white man in his stead, just for the kick of watching Dog's parents freak out over finding a strange cadaver in their bathroom, but Dog said no, he didn't think so. The Doze, he said, was generally that sadistic only on Sunday afternoons, when such bloodletting had a direct effect upon the National Football League's AFC Western Division standings.

Big Joe and I were relieved to have reached the common conclusion that our son was not a murderer, of course, but that isn't to say that either one of us was satisfied that he had told us everything he knew. We both knew better than that. Because getting the truth out of Dog—even for me—is a lot like drawing water from an old, rusty pump: you never get more than a thimbleful at one time. And sometimes, the more you pump, the less you get. Joe and I shared a strong suspicion that there were parts of the whole truth that Bad Dog was still not telling, but after some discussion, we agreed that it probably had little or nothing to do with the actual circumstances of Bettis's death, so we decided not to worry about it. Experience had taught us that we'd find out what it was soon enough, in any case. All we had to do was watch the boy and wait.

It was a tactic I had more patience for than Joe, as you might expect, but that was just too bad. I hadn't brought Dog and his four siblings into this world alone, I reminded my husband; I had help. So Joe got to play our son's shadow first. I kicked him and Dog out of our hotel cabin only minutes after Dog's second interrogation of the day and told them both not to come back for at least two hours, so that I could nap in relative peace. I hadn't treated myself to a decent midday snooze in over three days, and exhaustion was catching up with me. I collected Joe's key to our room, tossed a handful of guidebooks and sightseeing brochures in his direction, and closed the door on all his and Dog's objections.

Two minutes later, I was asleep.

Less than ten minutes after that, however, I was awake again.

Somebody was knocking on the door, lightly but incessantly. Making a very polite nuisance of themselves. I thought it might be Joe, until I realized the knocking had been going on for some time now, and the door was still on its hinges. And I knew it couldn't be Bad Dog, because I had yet to hear a single "Yo, Moms! Wake up in there!"

So I got up to see who it was.

There was no peephole in the cabin door, but by peeking through the drapes at one of the windows flanking it, I was able to see two men standing out on the porch, young, well-dressed white men I did not recognize. One appeared to have a camera dangling from his neck.

"Who is it?" I called out, trying to sound like an angry grizzly roused from hibernation.

They both turned toward the window at the sound of my voice, and instinctively I withdrew from it. One of them actually came over to the window and pressed his face to the screen, trying to get a look at me, but when he realized he couldn't, he quickly backed away again.

"Mrs. Loudermilk?" someone asked tentatively.

"I asked, who is it?" I said again, turning up the grizzly in my voice.

"We're reporters, Mrs. Loudermilk. We'd like to ask you and your husband a few questions, if we could. Would that be all right?"

Reporters. Of course.

Ever since the news of Geoffry Bettis's death had begun to circulate about the Canyon's trailer park two days ago, Bad Dog, Big Joe, and I had been besieged by an army of these bloodthirsty, soulless media creatures. In the beginning, we accommodated each and every one of them as best we could, answering what questions we had the answers to and graciously declining the rest. We saw no harm in it; what did we have to hide? But then the questions became more and more invasive and crude, and all the attention we were receiving began to lose its charm. When one of the local papers finally ran a story on us with a headline that read, "CANYON MYSTERY COUPLE LIED TO AUTHORITIES"—making a federal case out of the fact that I had told Detectives Crowe and Bollinger I was fifty-one, and Joe had told them he once played varsity basketball with Elgin Baylor back in high school—that was it. We all stopped talking to reporters altogether.

(Oh, and by the way—Joe's lie was more outrageous than mine, and by a wide margin. He and Baylor shared the same graduating class in high school, all right, but Joe was cut from the *junior* varsity basketball team after only three practices. The closest he ever came to actually playing with Baylor was, in his later role as the team's locker room attendant, flipping Baylor a towel in the shower room.)

Anyway, after a while of getting the Loudermilk cold shoulder, the vultures got the message and stopped circling about us. I figured our celebrity status had worn off for good.

But no. Here they were again. Two fresh new faces, at least, but insidious newshounds just the same. I knew that if I talked to these jokers, they would ask nothing but embarrassing questions, and distort my answers to those questions, and generally just make a mockery of what I had to say in tomorrow's morning paper.

So why did I go to the cabin door and open it? you ask. Because I *liked* having reporters scurry after me like paparazzi chasing down Liz Taylor—that's why. What did you think?

"My husband and I have nothing to say," I said, confident that neither man would take me at all seriously.

"Mrs. Loudermilk?" the one without the camera asked.

They were both dressed to the nines. That struck me right away. Perfectly tailored Armani suits in a matching charcoal gray, razor-cut silk ties, and high-gloss wing-tipped shoes—the full *GQ* treatment, everything first-class. Cub reporters, these guys weren't.

"I told you my husband and I have nothing to say," I said again.

"Mrs. Loudermilk, please. This will only take a moment, I promise you." It was the one without the camera again. He was the taller of the two, and the more handsome, though neither man looked like anything a bright girl would shove off the love seat in the family parlor. "My name is Ray, and this is Phil." He extended his hand, amber eyes sparkling. "Phil and I are doing a story on the Geoffry Bettis murder case. But I imagine you already guessed that."

I shook his hand, but only indifferently. "That's an Instamatic camera," I said, staring at the tiny little thing tethered to the neck of the one just introduced to me as Phil.

Both men followed my gaze before Phil looked up and shrugged his wide shoulders, apologizing. "My Nikon's in the shop, ma'am," he said.

"You gentlemen are from a newspaper?"

"Yes ma'am," Ray said.

"The *Sentinel*," Phil said.

"Aren't you kind of late?" I asked them. "I mean, all the other papers talked to Joe and me two days ago."

"Yes ma'am," Ray said. "That's true. But that's because Phil and I are doing a different kind of story than the other papers. We're doing what's called in the trade a 'follow-up.' "

"A follow-up," Phil agreed, nodding.

"A follow-up's a more in-depth look at the people involved in a story. A more personal look, if you will."

"More personal," I repeated.

"Yes ma'am. In other words, we don't so much want to know what happened as we want to know why and how it happened. It's the human drama we're after here, not just the cold, hard facts."

"The human drama. Exactly," Phil reiterated, head bobbing up and down.

"For instance," Ray went on, "we'd like to know what exactly was the nature of your relationship with Mr. Bettis before his death. Were you and your husband friends of his? Old business acquaintances? What?"

"We didn't *have* a relationship with Mr. Bettis," I said impatiently. "We'd never even heard of the man until the day we found his body in our bathroom.''

"I see."

Ray fell silent, trying to find a tactful way to pose his next question. After a moment, he said, "I hope you'll forgive me if this sounds disrespectful, Mrs. Loudermilk, but I find that rather difficult to believe. I mean, this is a big park." He swept his right hand in a wide arc before him to illustrate the point. "Mr. Bettis could have been killed in a thousand and one different places. But he was killed in your trailer. Sitting on your private commode. Now, there has to be a reason for that, don't you think?"

"There may be a reason for it," I said, "but if there is, neither my husband nor I know what it is."

I watched him toy with the idea of pushing me even further on the subject for a brief moment, before he said, "Okay. Stranger things have been known to happen, of course. We'll move on to our next question: What did Mr. Bettis say to you or your husband before he died? Anything?"

"Mr. Bettis was already dead when we found him. Haven't you read your own newspaper?"

"Please don't misunderstand, Mrs. Loudermilk. We don't mean to imply that you or your husband have been anything but honest with the press or the authorities regarding Mr. Bettis's death. In fact, we're certain you've both been entirely truthful in the matter. However . . . you've now had two days to think about what happened—to review things in your mind, if you will—and we just thought you may have remembered a few things that you'd forgotten or overlooked initially. You see?"

"You think we're senile," I said.

"No, no, no! Absolutely not!"

"Absolutely not," Phil said, shaking his head at the absurdity of the thought.

"You're not taking any pictures," I told him, suddenly getting a little worried.

"Huh?" He looked down at the little black plastic camera resting against his chest, appearing to have completely forgotten it was there, and said, "Oh. Well. I was waiting for your husband. We want to get the two of you together."

"Is he here, by the way?" Ray asked, taking a step toward me and the cabin door.

"Yes. But he's asleep," I said, moving to further block the open doorway with my body.

"What about your son? Theodore, is it? Is he here?"

"Yes. But he's asleep too."

"Ah. What a shame."

He tried to make an innocent gesture out of it, but as he straightened the knot on his tie, Ray took a quick look around, clearly making sure the three of us were alone. I had seen very unreporterlike muscles bulge beneath his coat sleeve when his arm moved. "Look, Mrs. Loudermilk," he said, showing me his perfect teeth again. "I get the sense that you don't trust us. So you're holding back on us a little bit. Is that possible?"

He took another small step forward, and this time his friend Phil the Photo Hound followed suit.

"I think I've said all I'm going to say to you gentlemen," I said nervously, backing slowly into the cabin. "I'm sorry."

But they had both advanced upon me yet another step,

when someone behind them said, "Yo, what's up?" to freeze them in place.

It was Bad Dog, drenched in sweat and covered with dust, his hair as wild as a four-year-old Brillo pad and his clothes a disheveled, ill-fitting mess. He looked like a psychopath on holiday.

In other words, he was beautiful.

He stepped up on the cabin's porch, placing himself right where I hoped he would—between me and my two visitors—and, grinning, asked, "Everything okay?"

Ray and Phil shot a glance at each other, wondering how I was going to answer that.

"Everything is fine, Theodore," I said, smiling at the two alleged reporters before me with the smug over-confidence of a don in the company of his hoods. "This is Ray and Phil. They're reporters from the *Sentinel*."

Ray and Phil nodded at my son officiously.

"That's an Instamatic camera," Bad Dog said, staring at Phil.

"His Canon's in the shop," I said. "Or did you say it was a Minolta?"

Phil didn't say anything.

"It's a Nikon," Ray answered for him, no longer finding it necessary to smile.

"I thought we weren't talking to reporters anymore," Bad Dog reminded me.

"We're not. In fact, that's exactly what I was explaining to these two when you walked up." I turned to Ray. "Wasn't I?"

Ray paused a moment, then reverted to the electric smile. The snake who lured Eve into sampling the apple could not have had a better one. "Yes ma'am. You certainly were." He lowered his head in Phil's direction, and the two fashion plates stepped down off the porch. Looking back one last time, he said, "I'm sorry you chose not to talk with us, Mrs. Loudermilk. It would have made our job so much more painless if you had. Believe me."

I was going to say, "I'm sorry too," but he and his partner were walking away by the time I could get my mouth to move. I wasn't sure, but it seemed to me I had just been presented with a thinly disguised threat.

Only when the pair had completely disappeared from view did I turn to my son and give him a big, smothering hug.

"What was that for?" Dog asked when I finally released him.

"For being my son. Is there anything wrong with that?"

"For being your son? I've been your son all my life, and it's never turned you mushy before. Unless you were bailing me out of jail, or somethin'."

"Let's just say having a dead ringer for the Antichrist in the family sometimes comes in handy, and leave it at that. All right?" I looked out expectantly in the direction from which Dog had come. "Now. Where is your father?"

Dog shrugged. "Still down there somewhere, I guess. He's comin'." He started to enter the cabin, but I put a hand on his chest to stop him and turn him around.

" 'Still down there somewhere'? Down *where,* Theodore?"

"You know. In the Canyon."

"In the Canyon?"

"Yes ma'am." He tried again to go inside, but my hand went right back to his chest to halt him in his tracks.

"You left your father down at the bottom of the Grand Canyon, Theodore?"

"He's not at the bottom, Moms. He's about three quarters of the way down. That's as far as he would go before demandin' we turn around and head back up."

"And you just left him there?"

"I didn't mean to. But see, there was this mule team on its way down, and I went around it, but he wouldn't. 'Cause, see, the trail's really narrow in places, and he got spooked once when he almost slipped, so—"

"Go back and get him, Theodore. Right this minute!"

"But—"

"Boy, if you're still standing here when I get this shoe off, you and me are gonna be in the news all over again. You understand what I'm saying?"

I started pulling the shoe off my right foot.

"Okay, okay! Damn!"

Bad Dog scurried off.

"And take him down some water!" I called after him, waving my shoe at his back. When I was sure he was doing as he'd been told, I started back into the cabin, yawning, and kicked my other shoe off, once more drawn inexorably toward my afternoon nap.

Until, that is, I remembered Ray and Phil.

Dog hadn't taken three steps down the trail into the Canyon when I caught up with him.

• • •

Several hours later, as I was soothing Big Joe's furrowed brow with a freshly dampened washcloth, I asked him what he thought.

"I'll tell you what I think," he said, trying mightily to raise his weary head from the pillow on the bed. "I think he thinks there's money to be made in my demise, that's what I think! I think he thinks he's got some kind of inheritance coming when I kick the bucket! But he's in for a rude surprise!"

"Joe, I'm not talking about Theodore."

"You hear me, boy? There ain't no profit in killing me, all right? Makin' a widow out of your mother ain't gonna make you so much as one thin dime!"

Glued as usual to the television set, Bad Dog just sat on the floor at the foot of the bed and said nothing, either too big or too dense to be insulted by his father's accusations. He knew as well as I did that Joe was just blowing off steam. Joe had been tired and dirty when we'd come upon him less than a quarter mile from the top of the Canyon trail, but other than that, he'd been no closer to death than I was. He was in too fine a shape for that. Still, he had been furious, and I for one fully understood why.

He hadn't liked how Dog had just left him behind down there, like an old cripple too slow for a young pup to wait on.

Dog hadn't meant it that way, of course, but that's how Joe had taken it nevertheless. I could see the hurt in his eyes all during the climb back up to our cabin. So I'd run a warm bath for him as soon as we walked in, and laid out his favorite pajamas, trying to assuage his wounded pride with a little old-fashioned wifely nurturing. I knew it wouldn't quiet him completely, but I suspected it might reduce his griping to a mere grumble in an hour or so, and I was right. The big baby wasn't doing anything more now than thinking out loud, no real sting left in his tone.

For some men, bellyaching was therapeutic.

"Joe, enough about Theodore. I'm talking about those reporters. Phil and Ray."

"What about 'em?"

"Well, for one thing, I don't really think they *were* reporters. You heard how they were dressed."

"Yeah."

"And that camera the one named Phil had. Who ever heard of a newspaper photographer taking pictures for his paper with a fifteen-dollar Instamatic camera?"

Joe considered the question carefully, then nodded his head. "Okay. So they weren't reporters. What do you figure they were?"

"Baby, I was hoping you could tell me. You're the ex-policeman, not me."

He nodded his head again, seeing my point. "Well, I didn't see them, but based on your description . . . I'd be tempted to guess they were government men of some kind. Well dressed, well spoken. Polite. Except . . ." He let the thought fade away.

"Except what?"

"Except government men don't usually pretend to be anything else. They don't have to. They want to talk to somebody, they usually just flash their shiny badges and start leaning on people. They've got more weight behind 'em than anybody—why give up that kind of leverage just to play reporter?''

I didn't know how to answer that, so I simply shrugged.

"You say they tried to force their way in here?" Big Joe asked me.

"Yes. At least, it seemed to me that's what they were about to do, until Theodore showed up. I tell you, I've never been so glad to see that boy in my life.''

Bad Dog turned his head in my direction and grinned.

Frowning, Joe said, "Boy, you need a bath worse than I did. Go run some water in that tub and give your mother and me some privacy!''

The grin fell off Dog's face like the shingle from a roof, but he did as he was told. When he'd locked the bathroom door behind him, Joe looked at me and said, "He really pissed me off today, you know.''

"I know, baby. But you know he didn't mean to.''

"I was supposed to be watching him, and he gave me the slip. Five, ten years ago, he could've never done that, Dottie. Nobody could've.''

"I know.'' I smiled at him and ran my hand along the side of his head, feeling the gray hairs prickle my palm. "We're slowing down, you and me.''

"Yeah.'' His right hand was on my left shoulder, lightly stroking the skin beneath my blouse. It felt good.

"How long you figure he'll be in there?" Joe asked, a childish grin breaking out on his face.

"Not long enough. So forget it," I said, laughing.

"I can fix that door so he can't open it till we're ready for him to. How about it?"

"Joe, no!"

"Come on. What's the worst that can happen? We shock the boy a little bit. Hell, that might be good for him!" He leaned up on the bed to kiss me, and I kissed him right back. The old boy can kiss; he always could.

"You've got to be quiet," I told him.

"I will if you will," he said, laughing as he pulled back the covers on the bed for me.

And apart from an occasional giggle, we didn't make a sound for the next twenty minutes.

"You think maybe we should check on him?" I asked Joe when we were done, nodding at the bathroom door. Bad Dog had been every bit as silent as we had been over the last half hour.

"Naw. He's fine," Joe said, buttoning his pajama top back up. The contented expression glued to his face looked like something you'd see on a benevolent circus clown, and I had to laugh.

"Go ahead and laugh," he said, "but you'd better take a look at your own face in that mirror 'fore you do. See if you don't look just as dumb and happy as I do."

He chuckled as I went to the mirror above the dresser to see what he was talking about for myself. Sure enough, demanding center stage from my short, light brown Afro and round, generously freckled cheeks, the stupid grin was there, the same one I used to wear forty years ago, when we were teenagers just learning how fine loving sex could make us feel.

"See? What'd I tell you?" my husband teased. "Dumb and happy, just like me."

I waved my hand to shush him and gestured toward the bathroom door. I tossed a robe on and was gathering up my clothes from the floor when something caught my eye at the foot of the television set, where Bad Dog had been sitting less than an hour ago. It was a small notepad of hotel stationery and a pen, both bearing the same "Bright Angel Lodge" logo. Dog had apparently been scribbling on the pad as he watched television, writing the same thing over and over again:

Jeffrey Bettman   Jeffrey Bettman   Jeffrey Bettman

I handed the pad over to Joe. "Take a look at this," I said.

He examined the pad and said simply, "Uh-huh. Just as I thought."

"You know who this Jeffrey Bettman is?"

"No. But I know that's not him in our bathroom."

"Sounds very similar to 'Geoffry Bettis,' doesn't it?"

"Yeah. Very similar."

"I don't suppose that could just be a wild coincidence."

"That's not his handwriting, Dottie."

"No. It isn't, is it?"

Joe handed me back the notepad and said, "Put it back where you found it. Leave everything the way it was."

"He's copying that man's signature."

"Yeah." Joe nodded. "That's what it looks like to me."

"From what?"

"I don't know. But I'm gonna find out. Only this time, I'm not gonna bother askin' him. 'Cause, obviously, that's just a waste of time. We're ever gonna get to the truth about all this, we're gonna have to get it out of him the hard way. I see that now."

The sudden sound of more hot water being run in the tub startled me, and I turned, but Dog did not emerge from the bathroom.

"What do you mean, the hard way?" I asked, looking at Joe again.

"I mean we're not gonna find out anything by putting him on a short leash. We've tried that, and it doesn't work. It's like the old saying goes: 'A watched pot never boils.' Only way that boy's gonna lead us to the truth is by accident. Meanin' from now on, we've gotta let him go about his business alone, by himself, and let him think nobody's watching. Except that we will be, of course. Only from a distance this time."

I nodded, agreeing with him, and placed the notepad and pen in their original places on the floor as he had directed.

Our son emerged from the bathroom a few minutes later, one towel wrapped around his waist as he dried his hair with another. He was singing some rap song I didn't recognize, vocally re-creating all those *boomp-boomp, ba-da-thump, ba-da-thump* noises that kids today call music. Starting toward the bathroom to take my own bath, I watched out of the corner of my eye as he spotted the notepad on the floor, hesitated for a moment, then slid his right foot over the carpet nonchalantly to kick it under the bed, confident that he hadn't been seen.

Big Joe and I nodded at each other.

Ten minutes later, I lay stretched out in a tubful of lukewarm water, wondering if I ever wanted to get out. Because the truth about my son could not find me here in the bath; the truth was out there with him. Not knowing what that truth was, how innocent or how terrible, was upsetting in itself, yes, but there was some comfort in it. For horrible suspicions were still just suspicions, after all; horrible knowledge was something else entirely. Knowledge was real and inescapable; it could be a dream made solid, or your worst fears etched in stone.

And the knowledge of Bad Dog's role in the murder of Geoffry Bettis was just outside the door to my right, waiting for me to come looking for it with the dawn.

I didn't leave that tub until the water was too cold to stand a moment longer.

6

Thursday morning, we all ate breakfast together at the hotel restaurant, then went our separate ways. Or at least, that's what Joe and I led Dog to believe we did. We told him we were going to drive down into town to the amphitheater there to see some wraparound Grand Canyon film all the brochures claimed was a don't miss, and naturally, as we knew he would, Dog pleaded on bended knee not to join us. For appearance's sake, Joe went through the motions of demanding he come along, but after a few minutes, the two of us just threw up our hands in a show of joint disgust and let him be, allowing him to think he'd somehow finally won an argument with his father.

We drove our pickup all the way out to the park's front gate, then turned around at the loop there to double back. We parked in front of the visitors' center and walked the remaining hundred yards or so to the hotel, staying in the woods among the trees and off the foot trails so Dog wouldn't spot us if we ran into him coming the other way. Which, as it happened, is exactly what we did. Joe poked me in the ribs and pointed, and there Dog was: walking west along the edge of the main road toward us, his bushy head down and his eyes fixed on the earth ahead, moving like a man with a purpose.

Joe and I each found a tree to hide behind and watched as Dog followed the side road leading to the village proper. We let him build a decent lead, then followed slowly after him, moving up just a few steps at a time to keep the distance between us constant. There was a cafeteria, gift shop, bank, post office, and general store in the village square, but Dog gave us no clue as to which of the five was his destination until he hit the parking lot and began angling over to the post office. To say that that confused me would be an understatement. Here the boy hadn't written his mother a decent letter in over ten years, and the first chance in three days he had to be alone, he was sneaking off to visit a post office.

Or was he?

He was up on the post office's porch, seemingly ready to go inside, when he suddenly veered right and started for the little bank next door instead.

"Now, what does that boy want with a bank?" Joe asked as Dog disappeared inside, more thinking out loud than conversing with me.

"I don't know," I said, starting to feel a little light-headed. "But all he's been talking about since he came here is money. Money, money, money." I paused, almost afraid to go on. "Joe, you don't suppose—"

"No," my husband said quickly, shaking his head back and forth to defuse my unfinished thought. "He's not that crazy. I took his gun away, remember? A man can't rob a bank without a gun."

That wasn't true, and he knew it, but he was trying to dispel his own fears as well as my own, and I imagined he couldn't think of anything more reassuring to say.

"Well? Are you going in there after him, or am I?" I asked after a while.

"I'll go," he said. "You stay right here."

"Where? Out here in the middle of the parking lot?"

"No. Go over there by the gift shop." He pointed to show me the way. "And stay there unless I signal you to duck inside. Like this." He made a little bye-bye wave with his right hand.

I nodded to show him I understood, and then he was gone.

I took my designated position in front of the gift shop and turned back around to watch as Joe trotted over to the bank, narrowly avoiding a collision with a station wagon as overloaded with kids as it was piled high with luggage. The overweight driver behind the wheel shouted something ugly out at Joe, and Joe returned the favor, but that was as far as their altercation went. He didn't know it, but the driver was lucky; any other time, Joe would have taken a few minutes to show the loud-mouth just how far one of the sleeping bags tied to the station wagon's roof could be forced into a man's left ear. Or down his throat. Or . . .

I think you get the idea.

Anyway, Big Joe reached the bank's double doors, but did not go inside. He just stood outside and to the right of them to peer through their glass panels into the tiny bungalow's interior. It occurred to me eventually that that was all he could do; the building was so small, it would have been impossible to enter it without being seen by everyone inside, Bad Dog included. I had no idea what kind of view he had of Dog from where he stood, but I assumed it was good because he never moved an inch to improve it.

A long ten minutes passed. I didn't like the waiting, but at the same time, I was relieved by it. Whatever else our son was doing inside that bank, I realized, he wasn't trying to rob it. Joe would have rushed in to stop him by now if he were.

I had taken all the standing around I could take when Joe finally and abruptly backed away from the bank's doors to alert me that Dog was coming. But he never gave me his time-to-get-out-of-sight wave. He just retreated far enough from the bank's entrance to avoid being spotted when Dog appeared; then he slipped up behind our son as he started back across the parking lot in my direction. Dog was ripping open a medium-size manila envelope as he walked, showing all the patience of a child tearing into a gift on his birthday. He was entirely taken aback when Joe poked a finger in his left side, then began using his weight to guide Dog over to where I was standing, dancing uneasily on the balls of my feet. For a black man, Dog didn't have much color to begin with, but in the few short minutes it took him to be brought before me, I watched him turn as deathly pale as a nauseated albino.

"Hello, Theodore," I said. The chill in my voice could have frosted a drinking glass.

"Moms. Hey," he said, trying his best to make a

smile form on his face. "I thought—"

"You thought we were going into town. Yes, I know. Your father and I wanted you to think that, Theodore."

"Sure did," Joe said. "We set ourselves a little trap, and hell if you didn't walk straight into it."

Bad Dog looked from his father's face to mine, back to Joe's, then back to mine again, apparently trying to decide upon whose mercy he should throw himself. "Moms—"

"Moms, nothing. I'm ashamed of you, Theodore. We both are. We've given you every opportunity to tell us the truth about your involvement in Mr. Bettis's death, and all you've done is lie, lie, lie. You've lied to us, and you've lied to the police. But that's all going to come to a stop right now. And I do mean this instant!"

"But, Moms, I didn't *do* anything! All I did was—"

"Walk into that bank, pretend to be somebody named Jeffrey Bettman, and steal the contents of his safety deposit box," Big Joe said, fuming.

"Joe, he didn't," I said, aghast.

"Oh yes he did. I stood right over there and saw the whole thing!"

"Then he *did* rob Mr. Bettis!"

"No!" Bad Dog cried. "I didn't rob nobody! All I did was take the man's wallet, that's all!"

"That's 'all'? Theodore, that's terrible!" I said.

"I guess you know where we're all goin' now, don't you, boy?" Joe asked him, sounding more like a cold and bullying cop than he had ever actually been. "Or do I have to tell you?"

He started marching Dog down the road, out of the

village, and I followed close behind them.

"Pops, please! Let's leave the police out of this, all right?"

"I think we've left them out of it long enough, Theodore," I said. "Don't you?"

"Moms, listen to me! I wasn't tryin' to steal nothin'! I was just tryin' to help you an' Pops get off the hook for Bettis's murder! I only got this stuff out of his safety deposit box 'cause I thought there might be somethin' in there could prove you guys didn't kill the man!"

"Oh, Jeez Looweez," Joe sneered, rolling his eyes skyward. I'd wondered when those wonderfully expressive "Jeez Looweezes" of his were coming.

"I swear, it's the truth! I was just lookin' for some *evidence!*"

" 'Evidence'? Evidence of *what?*"

"I don't know. I ain't had a chance to look in the envelope yet!"

Finally, Dog had said something to earn himself a reprieve. Big Joe stopped walking.

"He's right, Joe," I said.

"Dottie, don't even get started—"

"I know, I know. Whatever's in that envelope is none of our business."

"That's right."

"Even if it could clear us of the charge of murder."

"Yes. I mean, no. No! Woman, I told you not to get started!"

"Baby, I can't help it. I'm curious, and so are you. It's written all over your face."

"Say what?"

"Come on, Pops," Bad Dog told his father. "Give it up. You're an ex-cop, man, you can't help but be curious. It's in the blood."

Having Dog and me read his mind like an open book has always rubbed Joe the wrong way, but for once he didn't foam at the mouth refuting the accuracy of our perceptions. He merely sulked for a brief moment before holding out his right hand to Dog and saying, "Okay. Let's have it."

Dog grinned and gave him the envelope. We all huddled in a tight circle and held our collective breath as Joe lifted the flap and reached inside to withdraw its contents: three eight-by-ten black-and-white glossies and a pencil sketch on a lined piece of paper. We looked each item over carefully as Joe flipped through them, and then Joe said out loud what each one of us was thinking:

"What in the hell?"

The photographs were all different shots of a man going out to his mailbox; stepping out of his front door, moving down the walk, taking a handful of letters from the box. He was a white man somewhere in his middle to late forties, wearing a plain white T-shirt and a pair of khaki pants. He was trim and immaculately clean-shaven, with a wide band of scalp running front to back on the top of his head like a small highway. All in all he seemed very ordinary, except for one small thing: He looked scared. In all three photographs, his eyes were not on what he was doing so much as on his surroundings; it was as if he were expecting some kind of trouble to drop on him at any minute. The pencil sketch, meanwhile, was still more obscure: just a poorly drawn outline of someone's disfigured right foot. The drawing showed much of the third and fourth toes to be missing; the former was nothing but a tiny stub, and the latter was only marginally more than that. Their tips were identically angular, so that it seemed they had been trimmed simultaneously with a pair of garden shears.

"I don't get it," Bad Dog said. He took the envelope from his father and looked inside, but of course, it was empty.

Joe glared at him. "What's to get? You wanted 'evidence,' and you got it. Three pictures of a white man going out to his mailbox, and a drawing of someone's messed-up right foot. Proof positive none of us killed Geoffry Bettis."

I took the photos and sketch from my husband's hands and examined them myself. Written on the back of one of the eight-by-tens, I found a Flagstaff, Arizona, address I hadn't noticed before, but other than that, the material revealed nothing new to me. Certainly nothing that could be seen to help our cause, anyway.

"Come on, Dottie," Joe said. "We're wasting time. Let's get this boy over to the rangers' office before they come looking for him. It'll look better for him that way."

"Joe, this stuff has to mean *something*," I said, handing him the photographs and sketch so he could put them back in the envelope.

"Look. I don't care if it does or it doesn't. All I know

is, it's got nothing to do with us, and that's all that matters right now. So let's stop talkin' and start walkin', all right?''

''But why would a man put stuff like that in a safety deposit box at the Grand Canyon? Unless it was somehow very valuable?''

''I don't know, and I don't care. Hell, we should've never opened this envelope up in the first place! All we did was add another count to the charges they're going to eventually bring against us.''

''Joe—''

''You're gettin' on my nerves, Dottie. Okay?''

''But she's right, Pops!'' Bad Dog cried. ''Those pictures have gotta mean somethin'!''

''They do. They mean you've told your last lie in the state of Arizona. Now, let's go.''

He took Bad Dog by the arm and started marching him down the road again. In a last-ditch effort to change his mind, I stayed put, but I don't think Joe ever even noticed. He had finally taken all of Bad Dog's nonsense he could take.

And one way or another, he was going to get to the bottom of things.

''I was just about to call you people,'' Ranger Cooper said. ''I've got good news.''

We were standing out in the receptionist's area, shaking in our boots as we waited to be called inside to his office, when Cooper came out to greet us instead, grinning from ear to ear.

''I just got off the phone with the sheriff's office.

They say they've found Bettis's car. Seems some fellow robbed a convenience store down in Williams last night and was driving it when they picked him up this morning. They aren't sure, but they think they've got their man.''

His grin grew wider, fanning the bristles of his red mustache out like a peacock's feathers. It was starting to look cute to me again.

"What I'm trying to say, folks, is that you can all go home," Cooper said.

None of us Loudermilks knew what to say. Exoneration was not what we had come here to receive. We'd come instead braced for surrender, ready to make some embarrassing confessions and to suffer some painful consequences, and now we were being told that none of that unpleasantness would be necessary. We were free to go home.

"I don't understand," Joe said.

Cooper didn't know what to make of our lackluster reaction to his announcement. He just kept smiling, as if by making a happy face he could get the point across to us that something very good had happened.

"I said you can all go home. They've found Bettis's killer. See, the car—" He stopped, seeing that he still wasn't making a dent in our shared state of disbelief. Finally, he reached back for the knob on his office door and said, "Come on inside, folks. We can talk about it in here."

When we were all sitting down, the ranger asked, "Are you all okay? You look kind of funny."

Joe still had the envelope Bad Dog had taken from

Geoffry Bettis's safety deposit box gripped tightly in his right hand. Out of the corner of my eye, I watched him slide it quickly up into his lap and out of sight, hoping to do so before Cooper could take notice of it. "Funny? Really?" He looked at me, then at Bad Dog. Dog's mouth was hanging open like a castle drawbridge. "No. We're just surprised, that's all." Joe laughed as if relieved.

"Yes. We can't believe it," I said, following my husband's lead.

"I see," Cooper said. He was watching Bad Dog drool.

"You were saying they found Mr. Bettis's car," Big Joe said, using the comment as camouflage while he kicked the leg of our son's chair to bring him around.

"Yessir," Cooper said. "They say a rear window had been busted out and the ignition had been hot-wired. This guy they found driving it says he stole it from one of the parking lots here late Tuesday afternoon and never even set eyes on Bettis, but the sheriff's boys aren't buying that. They say this fellow's got a rap sheet as long as your arm, and the gun they took out of the car when they arrested him—the one he used in the convenience store robbery, apparently—was similar to the one that killed Bettis: a small-caliber thirty-eight. They won't know for sure that it's the right gun until they run it through ballistics, of course, but they seem pretty satisfied that it'll prove to be, sooner or later."

"So they're letting us go," I said.

"Yes ma'am. Soon as they get your trailer back up here, you people are free to leave."

"And when will that be?" Joe asked.

"Excuse me?"

"When will they get Lucille back up here? Today, tomorrow—when?"

"Oh, oh. Lucille, she's your trailer?"

"It's what we like to call her, yes," I said, so that Joe wouldn't have to look like an idiot all by himself.

"Well, they didn't give me an exact time, but I would think they'd have her back to you no later than Saturday afternoon. Just as soon as they can get her all back together, anyway."

Now it was my turn to say, "Excuse me?"

"Aw, Jeez Looweez," Joe said, groaning with a sudden sense of foreboding. "You mean to tell me they tore her down?"

"Well, sir," Cooper said, doing a fast and uncomfortable retreat, "not completely, no. That is, it's my understanding they were still in the process when Mr. Bettis's car turned up. How *far* into it they were when the detectives called them off, I don't know, but—"

"We're going down there to get her ourselves," Joe said, not issuing a warning but stating a plain fact.

"What's that?"

"I said we're not gonna wait for them to bring her back up here. We're gonna go down there and pick her up ourselves. First thing tomorrow morning. I don't want her leavin' Flagstaff till I've had a chance to look her over first. You got that?"

Flustered, Cooper said, "Well, sir, Mr. Loudermilk, I'm not so sure—"

"Look. Those people have had our trailer nearly two

days now, and I want her back—but not in pieces. If she's got so much as a bolt or screw missing, the time to find out about it is now, while she's still in their custody, not three days from now when we've taken her back out on the road. So we're going down there to get her. Early tomorrow morning. You can give us instructions on how to get there before we leave. All right?''

You could see from the look on Cooper's face that it wasn't all right, at least not with him, but he was observant enough to recognize that an argument with Joe at this point was only going to end with three Loudermilks locked up in a jail cell. So rather than say what was really on his mind, the ranger merely shrugged and said, ''Sure, sure. If the sheriff's boys don't mind doing it that way, I don't see why I should. I'll call 'em soon as you leave.''

''Good,'' Joe said. He stood up from his chair and, informing Cooper that our meeting had just been adjourned, turned to Dog and me. ''Let's go,'' he said.

We were filing out of the room, with Dog taking up the rear, when, at the last minute, Dog stopped, turned, and asked Cooper, ''Whatever happened to that big guy who got arrested yesterday? You know, the giant brother that went crazy in the trailer park?''

Cooper made Dog wait for an answer, apparently finding the question odd. ''Why? He a friend of yours?'' he asked.

''Who, him?'' Dog shrugged. ''No, man. I just saw 'im get busted yesterday, an' wondered what happened to 'im. Big cat like that sort of catches your attention, right?''

Again, Cooper sat on his answer awhile before letting us in on it. "We let him go. We only brought him in to ask him a few questions and give him some time to calm down. For one reason or another, the man got a little excited out there, and we thought it might be a good idea to detain him for a while. That's all."

"Then, he went home, huh?"

"Maybe. I don't know. We didn't remove him from the park, if that's what you're asking. We had no reason to."

"He looked like a football player or somethin'," Dog said, his disappointment in learning Dozer Meadows might still be around only barely showing.

Cooper gave him a blank stare. "I guess he did at that."

Dog was smart enough to close the book on the subject right there.

"Thanks, Pops," Bad Dog said when we had returned to our cabin.

Joe didn't even look at him. "For what?"

"For not blowin' the whistle on me. About that stuff I took out of Bettis's safety deposit box, I mean." He was trying to have a tender moment with his father, but Joe was making it difficult, kicking off his shoes and throwing himself upon the bed to let Dog and me know he would be asleep inside fifteen minutes.

"There wasn't any point," Joe said gruffly, arranging the pillows behind his head to his liking.

"But you could have turned me in anyway. I mean, what I did *was* against the law and everything . . ."

"Forget about it. You robbed a bank and scored three photographs and an outline of somebody's deformed foot. America's Most Wanted, you're not."

Joe laced his fingers over his stomach and closed his eyes.

"On the other hand, young man, you do have a lot of explaining to do," I said, while the opportunity to catch our son in a contrite moment presented itself.

"You mean about the wallet," Bad Dog said, looking at the floor.

"That's exactly what I mean, yes. What on earth possessed you to steal a dead man's wallet? How could you possibly do something so . . . so . . ."

"Moronic," Big Joe said, his eyes still closed.

"That wasn't the word I was looking for," I said, wasting a perfectly good glare on him. Turning back to Dog, I went on, "Something more appropriate would be a word like 'callous.' Or 'unfeeling.' Or—"

"Hard up," Joe interrupted again.

"That's two words," Bad Dog said.

"The point is, Theodore," I said, "that stealing from the dead is an unconscionable act. It's sick. And I cannot understand how any son of mine could be capable of such a thing."

"Moms, I told you: I've been runnin' for my life! I need a grand to pay the Doze's fine, and I need it fast!"

"So you picked the pocket of a dead man sitting on the toilet. You just bent down, reached into the pants around his ankles, and—"

"I didn't pick nobody's pocket! I found his wallet in the refrigerator!"

"In the *refrigerator?*"

"Yeah, in the refrigerator. Behind all the beers. I know it sounds crazy, but that's the truth. First thing I did when I came into the trailer was go to the refrigerator to get somethin' to drink, and there was the wallet, just sittin' there. Starin' at me. I thought it was Pops' till I looked inside an' saw Bettis's name on everything. Everything 'cept his receipt for the safety deposit box, anyway. Name on that was Jeffrey Bettman. Then, after I found his body in the bathroom—"

"Where is the wallet now, Theodore?"

"Huh?"

"The wallet. Where is it now?"

"I don't know. I tossed it into the Canyon."

"When?"

"Right after I took it. That same night, late."

"And it was empty?"

"No ma'am. I left everything in it 'cept for his safety deposit box key."

"And his receipt for the box, with the Jeffrey Bettman signature on it."

Dog paused, as if I'd suddenly shifted the subject from Bettis's wallet to Washington infighting. "Huh?"

"You forged his signature, Theodore. You must have had something with his signature on it to go by."

"Oh, yeah, his receipt. I forgot about that." He smiled and shrugged at me at the same time. The child's physical and mental coordination was uncanny.

"What about cash?" I asked him.

"Cash?"

"Yes, cash. How much cash money did you take?"

"Cash money?"

"You make me open my eyes, boy, I'm gonna close yours for good," Big Joe said, sighing.

Dog faced me directly, bravely staring down the barrel of his fate, and said, "Seven hundred dollars."

"Seven hundred dollars!" I cried.

Joe opened his eyes.

"Yes ma'am. Give or take a few. I don't have that much now, of course, 'cause I've been buyin' food an' drinks an' stuff, but—"

"You mean to tell me you've been walking around here with seven hundred dollars in your pocket all the time you've been begging your father and me to loan you a thousand?"

"Yes ma'am."

"And you don't see anything wrong with that?"

"You mean, do I see anything wrong with askin' you guys for a thousand when I already had seven hundred?"

"That's the question, yes," I said.

He made a show out of thinking his answer through. "Well, not really." He shrugged. "I mean, I was gonna need some kind of *spendin' money* when we got to Pittsburgh—"

I immediately went to the dresser and started rummaging around in the right-hand top drawer for my good belt.

"What'd I do now?" Bad Dog cried, genuinely dumbfounded by this reaction. "What?"

"I'm about to show you. You just wait right there a minute," I said.

"All right, all right, so I was bein' a little greedy! I should've just asked you guys for three hundred bucks, not for the whole thousand."

"Damn straight," Joe said, just as I pulled my belt out and slammed the drawer shut.

"But if I'd done that, an' then found out the Doze wanted more'n his fine money to call us even—what was I gonna do then?" Dog asked.

"Take your lumps. Like a man," I said.

"Moms, the Doze doesn't leave you with 'lumps.' He leaves you in pieces. You think I'd've done all the things I've done if he didn't?"

He had the appearance of someone about to cry. I knew he wasn't, of course, but I also knew that this was as close as Dog ever came to real remorse; his heart wasn't heavy, but his conscience was annoying him.

What can I say? It touched me.

"Moms, I'm sorry. But this guy scares the hell out of me. You saw him yesterday. He's *crazy*."

"Maybe so. But that's no excuse, Theodore. None whatsoever."

"I know. I know. I'm sorry."

"Well, sorry's not going to cut it. You have to promise me from this moment forward that you are never going to lie to your father and me again, ever. About *anything*."

"Yes ma'am."

"And that goes for stealing, too."

"Yes." He nodded his head energetically.

"All right, then," I said, satisfied. Dog stepped forward and hugged me, and I hugged him right back, hard.

"You mean to tell me you're not gonna whip that boy's behind?" Joe asked, disappointed.

I looked at him and laughed. "No. I'm not."

"Hell," Joe said, and then he fell sound asleep.

7

The drive down to Flagstaff was a dull one.

For the first thirty-five miles or so leading out of the Grand Canyon, Highway 180 was just a two-lane swath cut through the Arizona flatlands, a colorless stretch of geography memorable only for its formidable monotony. Patches of piñon pine and Utah juniper trees interrupted this trend occasionally, but you had to be paying close attention to notice. When you finally came upon a large tourist trap overrun with giant Flintstones characters, Highway 180 turned east toward Flagstaff and left State Highway 64 to continue on south toward Williams. The change in direction made for more interesting scenery along 180, it was true, but only marginally; once you had taken in the snowcapped splendor of Humphreys Peak looming to your left, and admired the walls of ponderosa pine and aspen trees that eventually surrounded you on both sides, you were soon back to counting the minutes before a Flagstaff City Limits sign made an appearance.

This was more of a problem for me than it was for Joe, of course, because Joe had the distraction of driving to keep him company. And Dog, well, beautiful scenery

105

or the lack of same has never much mattered to him; on trips of any duration, he's usually asleep in a car before the click of his seat belt fastening has stopped echoing in his ears.

So what, you might ask, did I do in the cramped cab of a pickup truck to fend off boredom while my youngest son slobbered on my right shoulder, and my husband peered intently at the alternating white and yellow lines splitting the road ahead? I read three issues of *People* magazine before studying the contents of Geoffry Bettis's safety deposit box one more time. What else?

"This drawing has to mean *something*," I told Joe, referring to the crudely sketched outline of someone's grotesque right foot.

"You keep saying that," Joe said wearily.

"I can't help it. I keep thinking I've seen a foot like this somewhere before. I just can't remember where."

"Well, don't look at me. I've got beautiful feet."

"This doesn't look familiar to you?"

"No."

"And he doesn't either?" I asked, referring to the three odd monochromatic photographs of a stranger visiting his mailbox.

"No. Why should he?"

"Because this stuff *means* something, Joe. It has to."

Big Joe just made a disgruntled sound deep in his throat.

"You don't think it does?"

"It's not that. It's just that I'm past caring whether it does or not. What Bettis did and who killed him was only my concern while we were being held in connection with his murder, Dottie. Now that we're not, I couldn't care less about the man, or anything pertaining to him. All I want to do now is pick up Lucille and head east.''

''But, Joe—''

''I know, I know, he died in our trailer. But so what? We didn't put the man there. He invited himself in. Why should we feel responsible for him?''

''I didn't say we should feel responsible for him. All I meant was, I'd hate to leave here for good without finding out what happened to him, and why. And I should think you'd feel the same way.''

''Because I was a cop.''

''No. Because you were a *good* cop. Someone who was never satisfied with just a suspect, or a motive. You needed to know the *truth* about things. Good or bad.''

''That was my *job,*'' Joe said. ''This isn't.''

''No, but—''

''They have a suspect, Dottie. They'll get the truth out of him, sooner or later. And they aren't going to need our help to do it, believe me. Besides—'' He finally took his eyes off the road to look at me directly. ''We're already more involved in their investigation than wisdom says we should be. It's just lucky for us they don't know it yet.''

He glanced at the four items in my lap to make sure I got his meaning.

''You mean, if this stuff ever became relevant to their case . . .'' I said.

''We'd be up the creek without a paddle. Yeah. One way or another, they'd connect Dog to that safety de-

posit box, and that would be that. Even if they couldn't
pin Bettis's murder on him, the boy's committed enough
other crimes to get himself put away for fifteen years.
And us about half that for covering up for him.''

He let me think that over for a while, knowing I could
sit there for an hour and never come up with any line
of discussion to counter his reasoning. He was right.
Dog had put us all in a very precarious position, and
there was no greater evidence of that than the photographs and line drawing I held in my hands. The longer
they were in our possession, the longer they represented
a threat to our freedom; rather than pore over them like
Sherlock Holmes inspecting a heel print, I should have
lowered a side window thirty miles back and tossed the
whole works onto the highway.

And yet . . .

''What are you thinking?'' Big Joe asked. I'd been
silent for several minutes now, and he'd apparently seen
something in my expression he didn't like.

I turned to face him. ''What?''

''I said, what are you thinking? I can see and hear the
wheels turnin' from here.''

''What wheels?''

''We've gotta get rid of that stuff, Dottie. Soon as we
get into Flagstaff. You understand? We should've never
kept it around this long.''

''I thought you wanted to know what I was thinking.''

''I've reconsidered. Men can do that too, you know.''

''I was just thinking that maybe there's a way to in-
sure ourselves against prosecution if worse comes to
worse and, God forbid, they do come looking for us.''

"Yeah? And what way is that?"

"Well, by finding out what this means." I lifted the photos and drawing off my lap to gesture with. "How it's important."

"Nobody said it was important but you, Dottie."

"I know, I know. But if I'm right, and it did turn out to be important, and they were slapping the handcuffs on us . . . well, I just thought it might be a point for our side if we could tell them how this all fits in. You know, how it points to Bettis's murderer."

'They already have Bettis's murderer," Joe said.

"Do they? They have a man who was driving around in his car, yes, and a gun that may or may not have been the one used on Bettis. But that doesn't mean they have Bettis's murderer. Does it?"

"Dottie—"

"Look, baby," I said, raising my voice to be heard above the din of Bad Dog's snoring. "All I'm saying is, we're going to be down there in Flagstaff anyway, right? What can it hurt for us to look up Bettis's address in the phone book so we can pay our respects to his widow?"

Big Joe gave me a long, thoroughly disapproving look, and then stopped talking to me altogether.

I took that to mean okay.

Naturally, less than an hour later, Joe found something about Lucille to complain about.

As one might have predicted, the Coconino County Sheriff's Department forensics team had decided to start their dismantling work in our trailer's bathroom, since that, after all, was where Geoffry Bettis had died. Joe and I had been relieved to learn that the bathroom was as far as they had had time to get, but that turned out to be small consolation to Joe the first time he tried to flush Lucille's chemical toilet. It seemed the lab technicians who dismantled it had reinstalled a rubber seal improperly, so that the bowl was leaking water from something Joe kept referring to as "the mechanism." No one, including myself, had noticed the leak but him. Which was typical.

It was well after one in the afternoon before he was happy with Lucille's condition. While Bad Dog and I sat around drinking coffee and assorted canned sodas, Joe reassembled the toilet bowl himself before proceeding to inspect every inch of our trailer for similar nerve-grating flaws, paying no heed at all to the lab boys' constant assurances that nothing outside of Lucille's bathroom had been touched.

Throughout this ordeal, Detectives Crowe and Bollinger bit their tongues and played gracious, apologetic hosts, humoring Joe with only minor objections and basically ordering everyone else to stay out of his way. They weren't saying much about it, but they were obviously quite content with the case they had built against the armed robber they picked up driving Geoffry Bettis's car. Otherwise, I knew, they would hardly have been so anxious to treat us like innocent bystanders they'd been fools to ever suspect. Suspicion wasn't something policemen moved intact from one person to the next unless someone came along who finally seemed to deserve it all; that Crowe and Bollinger no longer appeared to have the slightest doubt about our innocence spoke volumes about how convinced they were of their latest suspect's guilt.

But, like I said, they weren't saying much about it. In fact, they weren't saying anything at all.

"I'm afraid we can't discuss that, Mrs. Loudermilk," Bollinger said at one point, after I'd asked him if their suspect had a name.

"You can't tell me his name?"

"No ma'am. I'm sorry."

"We understand he was driving Mr. Bettis's car when you picked him up."

"Yes ma'am."

"And that he was armed with a gun?"

"That's right."

"And this gun, it was the same one that killed Mr. Bettis. Is that right?"

"Again, Mrs. Loudermilk, I'm afraid I can't answer that question at this time. I'd really like to, but I can't."

He didn't know it, but there was no need for him to apologize; the slight glimmer of contentment that had shone in his eyes upon hearing my question had answered it perfectly. The results of their ballistics tests were in, and the two guns were indeed one and the same.

"Has he confessed to the crime?" I asked, determined to take Bollinger to the limit of his patience.

"Mrs. Loudermilk—"

"I just wondered if he's confessed, that's all. I only want to know what to tell all our friends back home when they ask me the same questions I'm asking you."

I smiled, and that seemed to buy me at least another smidgen of his generosity.

"No," he said, gulping at his coffee while his eyes remained glued to the lunchroom door, just in case his partner Crowe should come bursting in at any moment to catch us discussing the undiscussable. "The suspect has not yet issued a confession."

"Then, how can you be so sure—"

"That he did it? Easy. By listening to him try to explain himself. How he stole the car up at the Canyon, and just happened to find a loaded gun under the passenger seat. Would you believe a story like that, Mrs. Loudermilk? Do you know anyone that would?"

"Well—"

"No, you wouldn't. And neither do we." He stood up from the table we were sharing and tossed his empty coffee cup into a nearby wastebasket, crushing it into a ball first. "By the way. That daughter of yours is a real charmer. The one out in California? The lawyer?"

"Oh. You mean Mo?" I'd forgotten she had said she was going to give Crowe and Bollinger a call.

"I guess that's her. She told us her name was Maureen. Maureen Doubleday, attorney-at-law."

I laughed. "Yeah, that's our Mo. Doubleday is her married name."

"I see."

"I hope she didn't give you and Detective Crowe too hard a time."

He shook his head. "Naw. We hear that kind of language all the time around here."

I laughed again, and this time he laughed right along with me.

● ● ●

"Does this mean we can go on to Pittsburgh now?" Bad Dog asked, elated.

"Nobody's goin' to Pittsburgh," Big Joe said. "At least, your mother and I sure as hell aren't. We're goin' to Texas. Or Louisiana, maybe."

"Later," I said.

"Not later. Now. Soon as we drop this boy off at the nearest Greyhound station."

Dog made a face. "You're gonna make me take a *bus* to Pittsburgh?"

"Nobody's gonna make you do anything. You can do whatever you want. Go to Pittsburgh on a bus, or Hawaii on a wookie board, makes no difference to me. All I know is—"

"You mean a *boogie* board," I said.

Joe turned, his train of thought completely derailed. "Boogie, wookie—" he started to say.

"Bugle boy of Company B," Dog said, and laughed.

I looked down into my bowl to keep from joining him and started in on my salad again.

We were having lunch at a Perkins restaurant only a few blocks away from the sheriff's station in Flagstaff. The boys were doing burgers while I was doing greens. Twenty minutes earlier, Joe had nearly finished the job of hitching Lucille back up to our Ford when I suggested we grab a bite to eat in town first, ostensibly to avoid the usual hassle of looking for a restaurant parking space big enough to accommodate a twenty-four-foot trailer home. I hadn't yet told him why I'd really made the suggestion, but I was working my way up to it, one inch at a time.

"You think it's funny?" my husband asked Dog, his dour mood impervious to levity. "Fine. Laugh and be merry. But see if you aren't just a speck in my rearview mirror inside of an hour."

Now *that* Joe found worth a chuckle.

"He's coming with us first, Joe," I told him, matter-of-factly.

"Goin' with you where?" Bad Dog asked, his voice dripping with apprehension.

"Nowhere," Joe said. "Your mother's mistaken."

"We're going to go see a house," I said to Dog. "And if we're lucky, and somebody's home when we get there—"

"No, Dottie. *No*," Joe said, scolding me like a puppy that had soiled the living room carpet. "We are not going to stick our noses another eighth of an inch into this mess, I told you that on the way down here!"

"No you didn't. I asked you what harm it would do for us to look up Mr. Bettis's widow while we were down here in Flagstaff, and you said none."

"I didn't say none. I dropped the subject."

"Exactly."

"Exactly?"

"Joe, when a woman drops the subject, she's closing it. When a man drops the subject, he's capitulating. You know that."

But Joe's head was already moving from side to side in a perfect, unhurried rhythm, conveying but a single thought in perpetuity: *No*. "It's not gonna happen, Dottie. The Bettis case is closed, there is absolutely no sensible reason for the three of us to keep snooping around in it.''

''But—''

''And don't give me any of that 'But what if they've got the wrong man' stuff again, either, because I don't wanna hear it. The guy was drivin' around in Bettis's car and pullin' holdup jobs with the gun that killed him. He couldn't be any guiltier if he'd been wearin' Bettis's Fruit of the Looms when the cops picked 'im up.''

''All right. So maybe they do have the right man. And maybe they don't. Either way, I still say we'd be smart to find out why Bettis had those pictures in his safety deposit box before the authorities do. Wouldn't we?''

''Dottie, for God's sake—'' Joe sighed.

''If you don't want to go, we won't go. I won't say another word. But San Antonio, Texas—or, worse yet, New Orleans, Louisiana—is hundreds of miles away from Flagstaff, Arizona, Joseph Loudermilk the Second—and that's an awful long way to go without hearing the sound of another human voice. Isn't it?''

I smiled and dug into my salad again.

A half hour later, Joe made a right turn out of the restaurant parking lot instead of a left, and another page was written in the Dottie Loudermilk Handbook of Shameless Bluffing.

We found the last address Geoffry Bettis would ever know in the telephone directory: 127 West Cottage Avenue. The pale yellow house the address belonged to was a tiny little thing on a tree-lined block full of tiny little things, all quiet as a monastery and engulfed in shade. A cobblestone wall ran waist-high around the Bettises' meager front yard, and two wrought-iron pillars dressed in white adorned their front porch. Old Route 66 lay just two blocks to the south; a block short of that, a long-dead neon sign peered over the trees from a height of fifty feet to promote its owner, the Sierra Vista Hotel.

I had to do some talking to get Joe and Bad Dog out of the truck, but when I finally did, we all stepped up on the Bettis porch together, the unease of the trespasser clouding our faces and making lead weights of our feet. Naturally, ringing the bell was a chore left to me. I pushed the button once, then twice, but nothing happened. If a chime or buzzer was going off inside the house somewhere, you couldn't tell by listening.

"Nobody's home. Let's go," Big Joe said as I tried the bell a third time. He was already off the porch and heading down the walk toward the street, Bad Dog scurrying right behind him.

I was coming off the porch to chase them down when we heard someone call out to us from the backyard, near the left side of the house: "I'm back here!"

It was a woman's voice; coarse as sandpaper and thoroughly indifferent. A little more energy, and it might have passed for rude. Following it, we went around the side of the house and through a chain-link gate to find a middle-aged woman in bare feet hanging clothes on a line, a cigarette threatening to tumble from one corner of her mouth. She was wearing an oversize white T-shirt and blue denim pants, and a time-worn scowl of disillusionment that could have been stolen from a gargoyle. Her dirty-blond hair was combed and pinned back in places, loose and unruly in others. Bending over to draw another piece of wet clothing from the wicker basket at her feet, she glanced at us briefly and said, "Can I help you?"

Again, her voice carried all the vitality and emotion of a heavy sigh.

"We're looking for Mrs. Geoffry Bettis," I said.

Her reaction to that was imperceptible; she just kept on hanging clothes. As if three black people she had never met came around the house to interrupt her chores at about this same time every day.

"Why?" she asked at last, working straight through the question.

"Well . . . We just want to offer her our condolences. That's all. For her husband, I mean."

She took a yellow blouse from the basket, shook the wrinkles and excess water from it, and hung it up on the line.

"You see, he died inside our trailer, and we just thought—"

She finally spun around, forgetting about her wash for the moment. I thought I had angered her, but then I realized she was simply annoyed; it was beginning to look as if a severe state of pique was the best this woman could do, passionwise.

"What?" She sucked hard on the forgotten cigarette hanging from her mouth, then withdrew it and blew out the smoke at a menacing angle, down and to her left. "What did you think?"

"Look, Mrs. Bettis," Joe said. "If this is a bad time for you—"

"You can come back later? Don't be silly. You're here now, let's talk."

She was looking at me.

"As I said before, we just wanted to offer you our condolences," I told her, edging toward rudeness myself.

"Because Geoff was killed in your trailer."

"Yes. I know that sounds strange, but—"

"Did you know my husband?"

"Did we know him? No. We just . . . *found* him."

"On our toilet," Bad Dog elaborated.

I shot him the same quick glance Joe did, then turned back to Bettis's widow. "We didn't know your husband, Mrs. Bettis, but we feel badly for him just the same. That's really all we came here to say."

"I see." She took another long drag on her cigarette and exhaled the smoke to the east. "Well, it's nice of you to be so concerned, Mrs. . . . ?"

"Loudermilk. Dorothy Loudermilk."

"Mrs. Loudermilk. Yes, well, it's nice of you to be so concerned, but you really shouldn't have bothered. Geoff was an asshole and a loser, and the world will be better off without him. Starting with me."

She smiled and started hanging clothes again.

"But he was *murdered,*" I said.

"Yeah. So I hear."

"You don't *care?*"

"Do I care? Of course I care. What kind of woman would I be if I didn't care?"

She was still smiling.

Joe edged over to take my arm and lead me away, but I just shook him off. "I don't understand," I said.

"Listen," Mrs. Bettis said, turning around again, and this time she had more to show me than a mild case of irritation. "You didn't know the man, all right? *I* did. For twenty-one years. So when I tell you he wasn't worth a minute of your grief, believe it. Nobody knows how worthless he was better than me. *Nobody.*"

She pitched her cigarette out onto her backyard lawn with the flick of a finger and eyed us, waiting to see if we would take her outburst as a hint to leave her in peace.

"Let's go, Dottie," Joe said to me firmly, reaching for my arm again. I didn't pull away this time.

"He was a loser," Bettis's widow went on. "A self-centered, misguided moron who thought he was a tycoon in the making. Twenty-one years I waited for that idiot to wise up, to stop dreaming his life away and start acting like a real husband to me, and a real father to our kids, but it never happened. *It never happened.*" She stopped to smile again, trying to make light of her bitterness, but her eyes were suddenly brimming with tears.

"Sorry we bothered you, Mrs. Bettis," Joe said, turning me around to guide me out of the yard.

"Wait a minute. I wanna show you something."

Mrs. Bettis left her basket of clothes behind and started for the back door to the little house, where she turned to find that we had made no move to follow her. "In here," she said. "Come on." She pulled the screen door open and disappeared inside.

Joe and I looked at each other.

"It wouldn't be a good idea," Joe said, shaking his head.

As if he thought that might actually stop me.

"This was Geoff's 'study,' " Mrs. Bettis said, making a little joke.

It was a bedroom without a bed, and that was just as well: Only a twin would have fit inside and left room for anything else. As it was, a small garage sale wooden desk and matching straight-back chair had the room's limited floor space all to themselves, and still the room seemed overcrowded. Adding to its claustrophobic effect were four walls someone had turned into virtual collages. Pinned, stapled, and taped to every inch of their surface was a mind-boggling display of paper: letters, posters, and newspaper clippings; magazine photographs, Post-it notes, and brochure pages:

A NaturLife bumper sticker.

A Worldway Products price list.

An American Scholastic Encyclopedia poster.

"My God," I said, without thinking, taking it all in.

Mrs. Bettis stood beside me in the doorway and brought another cigarette to life. "Yeah. Impressive, isn't it?"

A trio of bookcases were filled to capacity with books and magazines, their shelves bowed like rubber bands from the weight. A half dozen stacks of newspapers stood waist-high against one wall, staggering this way and that in an effort to remain upright.

"The king's domain," Mrs. Bettis went on wearily,

as Joe and I stepped fully into the room to examine its contents more closely. "Many a big deal was made here. Many a fortune lost."

She managed a short laugh before a smoker's cough broke it off.

"What *is* all this?" I asked her.

"You can't tell? It's research. Homework. What every genius reads just before making his first million. At least, that's what Geoff always said it was." She took a long drag on her cigarette and held the smoke in her lungs for a good minute. "I say it's *crap,*" she said when she finally exhaled.

I flipped through the magazines in one of the bookcases. They were mostly old issues of *True Detective* and *Entrepreneur, Money Matters* and *Business Opportunities.* The books, predictably, were all similarly themed self-help titles: *You're Better Than You Think You Are, Using Crystals to Maximize Your Earning Potential, Supercharge Your Selling Power,* etc., etc.

"There wasn't a single get-rich-quick scheme that man didn't try, at least once," Bettis's widow said. "You name it, he tried to sell it. Health food products, household products, homemade jewelry, encyclopedias, life insurance. Nothing was too idiotic for him to try, if getting filthy rich was the payoff. And when he wasn't trying to *sell* something, he was trying to *find* something, or someone, instead. For the finder's fee, or reward money. Of course, that was always a total waste of his time too." She allowed herself a little sigh before going on. "So you know what he'd do then? He'd just change philosophies. Like you and I change our socks, he'd change his spiritual beliefs. One day he'd be heavy into meditation, the next he'd be chanting to Buddha. First there was power in crystals, then in pyramids. I couldn't keep up. It was always something new. Existentialism, reincarnation, pseudo-Christianity . . .'' She shook her head and tried to smile. "What a *putz*."

She fell silent.

I watched her take her cigarette in and out of her mouth for a while, before I said, "I'm sorry."

"Yeah. You too." She used her hand to brush a wisp of gray hair back into place behind one ear, but it wouldn't stay put. "So maybe you understand now why I'm such a lousy grieving widow, huh?"

She turned and started down the hall, confident this time that we would follow. A moment later, we were all standing out on her front porch, working our way up to an awkward good-bye.

"Tell me something," Mrs. Bettis said, again addressing herself to me. "Why did you people come over here, anyway? Really."

"Because Moms thinks the cops have the wrong guy for your husband's murder," Bad Dog blurted out, finally ruining the blessed silence he'd been maintaining up to now. I could have killed him.

"We're gonna go on out to the car," Big Joe said with a smile, putting a viselike grip on the back of our son's neck before leading him away.

Mrs. Bettis watched them cross the street, then turned to me and said, "Is that true? You think the police have arrested the wrong man?"

"Not exactly. I'm just not sure they have the right

one, that's all." I shrugged noncommittally.

"Why not?"

"Because of these." I handed Mrs. Bettis the envelope Dog had taken from her husband's safety deposit box and waited for her to open it. "Your husband had these locked in a safety deposit box in a bank at the Canyon. We—I—think he was trying to hide them from somebody." I let her look the photographs and drawing over for a moment. "Do they mean anything to you?"

She looked up at me and shook her head. "No."

"I was afraid you might say that."

"You say Geoff had these locked in a safety deposit box? At the Grand Canyon?"

"That's right." I could already see her next question coming.

"So how did you get them, you don't mind my asking?"

"I'd just as soon not say," I said.

"Oh." She was looking right through me. "I guess the police haven't seen this stuff yet, then."

"No."

She just stood there, waiting for me to explain.

"Look. I'm a busybody. A strange man was killed in our trailer, and I feel like I have a right to know why. So, I've said some things and done some things without the authorities' knowledge I probably shouldn't have in order to learn the truth about what happened. I know it's none of my business, but I don't care. Sue me."

"Maybe I should," she said. When I started to walk off her porch in a huff, she said, "I'm sorry. I don't have any idea what this stuff is, or what it means."

I looked back to find her holding out the envelope and its contents for me to take.

"You don't recognize the man in the photographs?" I asked.

"No."

"What about the house?"

"Never seen it before." She shook her head.

"And the drawing?"

"What can I tell you? It's a *foot*. What am I supposed to make out of that?"

"You don't know whose foot it might be?"

"Besides someone with ugly toes? No. I don't."

I turned one of the photographs around and pointed to the address scrawled on the back. "What about this address? Do you know where this is?"

She took the photograph from my hand for a better look, then shook her head again. "No."

"But that is your husband's handwriting?"

She nodded. "Near as I can tell." She pushed the photograph back toward me. The look on her face said she was just about ready to do something else with her time.

"Mrs. Bettis, do you have any idea what your husband might have been doing up at the Canyon when he died? Did he go up there to meet someone, do you think?"

"I couldn't tell you. He didn't tell me anything, he just disappeared. That's why I reported him missing. I didn't know *where* he was. I just figured he was hiding somewhere. Or worse."

"Hiding?"

"That's right. Hiding. Laying low." She produced a small shrug. "We were in a little trouble with Uncle Sam, and they were starting to send agents around to the house. You know, trying to get a statement from him. So I thought maybe he'd just decided to go away for a while. Or he'd been picked up and thrown in jail, and nobody'd bothered to call and tell me."

"Uncle Sam? You mean the Feds?"

"I mean the IRS. Internal Revenue Service."

"Oh."

"Listen. Mrs. Loudermilk. It's been fun, but—"

"Of course. One more question, and I'll let you go."

She tipped her head to one side as if to say, *If you insist.*

"The shoe store where your husband worked. You wouldn't happen to have the phone number on you, would you?"

"I don't have it handy, but it's in the book. The name's Sherman's. Sherman's Shoes. Ask for Bob—he was Geoff's manager."

"Bob. Sure." I put the photos and sketch back in their envelope and shook her hand. "Thank you, Mrs. Bettis. You've been very kind."

"Forget it. You went a little out of your way, I went a little out of mine. We're even."

I smiled and started down her walkway toward the street.

"Hey!" she called after me abruptly.

I turned around.

"You really think they have the wrong guy?"

"I don't know," I said. "But I'm going to find out."

She took one last drag on her latest cigarette, then flicked it into her front yard and said, "Good."

8

"I don't have anything to say to you people," Bob said.

By "you people," he meant reporters. That's what I had told him I was when he'd finally come to the phone: a reporter. Maybe I should have represented myself as an IRS agent instead.

"I only have a handful of questions for you, sir," I said. "This will only take a moment of your time, I promise."

"Listen, I've said all I'm going to say about Geoffry Bettis, all right? I worked with him, that's all. I don't know anything about what happened to him, or why. Nothing."

"He never told you why he was going up to the Grand Canyon?"

"No. All he told me—" He cut the sentence off sharply, nearly giving something away. When he spoke again, several long seconds later, I could almost smell the fear that had come over him; his voice was leaden with it. "Look. Don't call me here again. You understand? I can't talk to you!"

He hung up the phone.

When I rejoined Bad Dog and Big Joe at our truck, Joe grinned at me and said, "Well? He wouldn't talk to you, right?" I guess he figured if he couldn't stop me from playing policewoman, the least he could do was gloat like a madman when things didn't go well.

"No," I said.

"Ha! What'd I tell you?"

"I don't mean, no, he wouldn't talk to me. I mean, no, that's not what happened. Exactly."

Joe frowned. "You wanna run that by me again?"

"In other words, he didn't say he *wouldn't* talk to me. He said he *couldn't* talk to me. That was the last thing he said, 'I can't talk to you!' " I fell silent for a moment, thinking about it. "That's a little strange, don't you think?"

"I think you callin' someone else strange is like the pot callin' the kettle black," Joe said.

He and Dog had a good laugh at that before we drove off.

Fifteen minutes later, we found a stationery store in town and bought a street map book for twenty dollars and some change. Dog thought we should just leaf through the book in the store until we found the page we needed, then rip it out discreetly and walk out, but I wouldn't let him do it. When Joe heard how much the book cost, he almost overruled me.

The address Geoffry Bettis had written on the back of one of the mysterious photographs he had placed in his safety deposit box was 505 West Fir, but when we followed the appropriate map to that address, there was no

home to be found there. Instead, 505 West Fir lay at the end
of a cul-de-sac high up in the northern hills of Flagstaff,
where a sparse collection of clean but ordinary single- and
two-story homes had been set into the towering woods.
Some of these homes stood close together, but most were
distant neighbors at best, separated by acres of trees and
vacant earth. The clearing that had been formed at 505
West Fir—or what a marker at the curb *said* was 505 West
Fir—was surrounded by such empty expanses on both
sides, but now there was no house on the site to enjoy the
isolation. There was nothing there but pine needles scat-
tered over a giant, level bed of dirt.

"What happened to the house?" Bad Dog asked,
scratching himself under one arm as he surveyed the
area.

"I don't know," I said. I was studying one of the
Bettis photographs again, comparing the stand of trees
in the background of each print to those I was actually
facing, and yes—when I finally found the right viewing
angle—I could see that we had come to the right place.
Albeit at the wrong time.

"All right. Enough is enough," Big Joe said. He'd
been standing over by our truck, arms crossed and lips
tight, refusing to take part in our examination of the
grounds.

"Joe, don't start. Please."

"Look. I went along with this nonsense as long as I
could, but this is as far as I go. It's time to give it up."

"Where did the house go, Joe? And the mailbox?"

"I don't know, and I don't care. *None of this is any
of our business!*"

"I think it is. I think it's *everyone's* business when a man is killed and his murderer is still out there on the street somewhere, waiting to kill again."

"Dottie—"

"You think this house just flew away, is that it? Like that old farmhouse in *The Wizard of Oz?* A tornado just swooped down the street yesterday and whisked it off, I guess."

"All right. So the house being gone is a little bizarre, I'll grant you that. But what if it is? Bizarre or not, none of this is leading us anywhere. We're not finding out anything useful, and we're just getting ourselves deeper and deeper into trouble with the law. Now, so far we've been lucky, and the local authorities haven't caught us snooping around, but sooner or later they're going to, and when that happens—"

"The shit is really gonna hit the fan," Bad Dog jumped in, anxious to lend a hand.

"Go wait in the truck," I told him.

"Yes ma'am."

When he had shuffled off, I turned to Joe and said, "I want to talk to some of the neighbors."

"No. We're getting out of here. Right now."

"I want to show them these pictures and ask them if they know who this man is. Or was."

"No, Dottie."

"Joe, if no one recognizes him, I'll call it quits. I promise." I started walking toward the nearest house on the east side of the street.

"Dottie!"

He had turned to give chase when we both saw him:

a black man the size of an aircraft carrier reaching into the open passenger-side window of our pickup truck to remove Dog from the seat.

"Come on outta there, you," Dozer Meadows said, laughing.

"Yo! Moms! Pops!" Dog shrieked at us, being drawn from the truck like a minnow on a short line.

"All right, all right! Put the boy down!" Joe ordered, racing me over to where the giant stood.

His prize in hand, Meadows held our son aloft with the greatest of ease and said, "This boy an' me got some business to take care of, old man. So butt out."

"You heard what my husband said! Put our son down!" I cried.

I was standing directly in front of him, my neck turned up at a ninety-degree angle so that I might see his face. It was like trying to spot the heliport atop the World Trade Center from down on the street.

"These are your folks, huh, Doggy?" Meadows asked Bad Dog casually, still not setting him down.

Dog tried to nod.

"Pleased to meet you," Meadows said, looking down at me again.

"Pleased to meet you. Now, please—put Theodore down before my husband has to hurt you. All right?"

It was a threat that Joe found far more terrifying than Meadows did, of course, but in one way or another it worked, because the big man finally did as he'd been told and dropped Dog back on his feet.

"Man, how the hell did you get here?" Dog asked Meadows, rolling his head around in a wide arc to get some feeling back into his neck.

"I followed you down here. What else?"

"You followed us down from the Canyon?" Big Joe asked.

"Yeah. I seen you an' my boy Doggy here comin' outta the rangers' office yesterday an' followed you to your cabin. I shoulda come in an' got 'im right then, see, but I thought maybe it'd be better if I could catch 'im alone somewhere later. You know, so as to keep my business with 'im private. Discreet. So I waited around an' just watched you guys, hopin' you'd split up sooner or later. Only you never did. Next thing I know, man, you all have jumped in your truck and headed for the exits. So what else could I do? I got in my car an' went after you."

"All the way down here to Flagstaff," I said.

"Yes ma'am." He nodded his tiny head at me. "I figured you guys'd have to go somewheres quiet and halfways deserted, I followed you around long enough. And this place is pretty quiet and deserted, right?" He grinned like a little boy. "It's like I said, ma'am. Your son an' me got us some serious business to take care of."

"I know all about that. His father does, too. And I can tell you right now, you're out of luck. We don't have your money, and neither does Theodore."

"Moms! Don't play like that!" Bad Dog said.

"So you can just go on back to the Rams and serve your suspension like a man, and leave my son and his parents alone."

"You mean the Raiders," Meadows said.

"What?"

"I play for the Raiders, ma'am. Not the Rams."

"The Raiders, the Rams—what's the difference?"

"The difference is, we play *football,* ma'am," Meadows said.

Big Joe started cracking up, and before I knew it, all three men were in stitches.

"Damn, that's a good one," Big Joe wheezed, wiping his eyes.

"I don't get it," I said.

It took several minutes for the laughter to wind down. When it finally did, Joe looked at Meadows and said, "Hey, look here, Dozer, man. What do you say we settle this dispute you have with Dog in a civilized manner? What do you say?"

The giant shrugged. "I'm all for that."

"The boy hasn't got your thousand dollars, and his mother and I don't have it either, but he does have a good-size piece of it. Don't you, Theodore?"

Dog wasn't sure where his father was going with this, but he nodded his head anyway.

"What's a 'good-size piece'?" Meadows asked him.

"About six hundred dollars," Dog said, and closed his eyes. He didn't want to see the blow that might be coming.

Meadows laughed, but not because he had just heard something funny. "Oh, no, no, no, no, no. Six hundred dollars? I don't think so, partner, no." He shook his head emphatically.

"But that's all I've got," Bad Dog said.

"Then you're about two hundred and fifty dollars short of gettin' outta here alive, my man. I'm sorry."

Meadows took hold of the back of Dog's neck again and squeezed.

I was about to take my first step to rush him when Joe said, "What do you say we split the difference?"

"How do you mean?"

"I mean, you just said you'd accept the six hundred he's got, plus another two hundred and fifty to let him go, right? So what if we gave you half the two hundred and fifty? A hundred and twenty-five bucks?"

While Meadows stood there and thought about it, I tried not to faint. Was this really Joe Loudermilk talking, offering up $125 of his hard-earned money for the life of our least cost-effective son? Or was he merely bluffing until a police unit could arrive in response to the report of four crazed black people threatening to riot that some horrified resident of this tranquil street had almost certainly called in by now?

"I gotta have at least two-fifty," Meadows said at last, shaking his head to decline Joe's bid.

"All right. We'll give you an even two hundred," Joe countered. "But that's it. Take it or leave it."

Meadows fell silent again, agonizing over his decision. I used the time to look his body over for a vulnerable spot of attack. The best I could come up with was an ankle. Perhaps if I wrapped my entire body around one, and held on for dear life, I could distract Goliath for a full half second before being kicked into the nearby woods like a soccer ball at a picnic.

And then again, perhaps not.

"I'd need the money now, not later," Meadows said to Joe.

"Sure. No problem."

The big man thought about it a moment longer, then set Dog free again and said, "Okay. We've got a deal. Where's the money?"

Joe turned to me and nodded his head, relegating the job of paying the man to me. I went to the truck to find my purse, and came back with $180 in cash. Bad Dog was still feeling around in his pockets when I handed the money over to Meadows.

"Oh-oh," we all heard Dog say.

"Oh-oh? Oh-oh, what?" Meadows asked.

"Theodore, quit messin' around and give the man his money," Joe said. "A deal is a deal, already."

But Bad Dog didn't comply. He just stood there frozen in time, a mask of abject terror solidifying on his face.

"Theodore, the money," I said, feeling myself edging toward panic.

"I don't have it," Bad Dog said.

"Say what?" Meadows asked.

"I mean, I don't have it on me. I just remembered. I left it back at the hotel."

"Theodore, why in heaven's name did you do that?" I asked.

"Because . . . I thought you guys might want to take it away from me. For safekeeping. And I didn't want the Doze here to catch me without it, so . . ."

"You hid it in our cabin."

"Yes ma'am. Inside the toilet tank in the bathroom."

"And then you forgot about it."

He shrugged, too embarrassed to answer the question any other way.

"But what's the big deal? We just go back and get it, right?"

"Uh-uh. No way," Meadows growled, shaking his shiny head. "The deal was, I get my money *now* or I get to tear your head off an' go home."

Before we knew it, he had Dog in a headlock and was tensing his muscles to twist it off like a stubborn bottle cap.

"Joe!" I screamed, looking to my husband for help.

"What? It's only the boy's head. Since when has he ever had any use for that?"

"Sorry, ma'am, but Doggy here has this comin'," Meadows said.

"No I don't! No I don't!" Bad Dog protested.

"All right. Go ahead," I told Meadows. "You want to hurt the boy, hurt the boy. We can't stop you. But you'd better be ready to hang up your Raider career for good if you do. You understand me? For *good!*"

That gave him reason to pause. He kept his arm firmly around Dog's neck, but we could see him relax his grip. He had probably thought about all the potential consequences of killing our son but that one: no more football. At least until next season, a whole twelve months away.

"Now," I said. "Stop all this foolishness and let's go on back to the Canyon to get your money."

"Back to the Canyon?" Joe said. "Now, hold on just one cotton-pickin' minute—"

"All right. I'll go," Meadows said, letting Bad Dog

loose. "But this time, he's ridin' with me. Not with you."

"Fine," I said. "Theodore, do what the Doozer says and go with him. Your father and I will drive ahead."

"That's Dozer, ma'am," Meadows corrected. "Like in 'bulldozer.'"

"Oh? I thought it was Doozer, as in, 'He's a real doozer.'"

"I'm not goin' back to the Grand Canyon," Joe said, still grousing.

I gave him a short, unappreciative glance, then turned to Meadows again and said, "Dozer, would you be good enough to escort Mr. Loudermilk to our truck? And see that he gets safely behind the wheel? He'll be doing the driving for us today."

"Yes ma'am. It'd be my pleasure."

The big man reached out for some part of my husband to latch onto, but too late: Big Joe was already in the truck's cab, all buckled up and ready to go.

Saying a lot of things under his breath I didn't think I'd want to hear.

____ 9 __

It wasn't practical, but we went and picked up Lucille from the sheriff's office before starting for the Canyon. I suspected just having her back in tow would have a therapeutic effect upon Big Joe, and I was right. He only ranted and raved for the first forty minutes of the ride, then ran out of steam and fell silent. Maybe the fact that I drifted off to sleep somewhere near the end of his tirade had something to do with that, I don't know.

In any case, we made good time. We were back on the Grand Canyon grounds by seven o'clock, just as the last layer of red was being swallowed up by a jet-black night sky. We had called ahead to make sure the trailer park still had a space available for Lucille, but we needn't have bothered; this was mid-October, well into the park's off-season, and accommodations were plentiful. We even ended up in our original space.

Naturally, the only thing Dozer Meadows had on his mind upon setting the parking brake of his car was getting his hands on his money, but I wouldn't let Bad Dog take him over to the hotel until I had made a phone call first. It had been a good two days since I had last talked to Mo, and I knew she deserved an update on our situation. She was a worrier, like me, and worriers tend to lose their minds if they aren't kept abreast of what's happening with their loved ones. Especially if all the news that fits is bad.

While Joe was busy fitting all of Lucille's hookups at the trailer park and baby-sitting Bad Dog and his over-size friend, I called our daughter from a pay phone in the lobby of the Bright Angel Lodge and told her every-thing that had happened to us since Wednesday night, when she'd last heard my voice. When I was through, she said exactly what I'd known she would say:

"Mother, I'm coming down there."

"No, Mo, you're not," I said.

"For heaven's sake, you've meddled in an ongoing police investigation! Impersonated a murder victim, forged his signature, stolen the contents of his safety deposit box, withheld evidence . . . Am I leaving any-thing out?"

"I don't know. Does lying to the authorities count?"

"There's nothing funny about this, Mother. If I don't fly down there to stop you now, you and Daddy will be pressing license plates until the end of the next cen-tury!"

"You're exaggerating."

"I am not."

"Listen, sweetheart. I didn't call you to get a lecture. I called you to hear your take on all this. What do you think is going on?"

She paused, took a deep breath, and said, "I have no idea. What you're describing is so . . . so . . ."

"Weird?"

"Yeah. That word will do. Weird." She didn't say anything for a moment, then: "Mom, you say the house in those photographs had been razed from the site? Completely?"

"There wasn't a trace of it to be found anywhere, Mo. Even the mailbox was gone."

"You couldn't have been at the wrong address?"

"No."

"You're sure?"

"I'm sure."

"Did you talk to any of the neighbors to see if they knew anything?"

"I wanted to, but your father wouldn't let me. Besides, your brother's homeboy Mr. Meadows showed up right about that time, and we had to leave."

"I see." Mo got silent on me again. "Well, listen, do you think you could find a fax machine around somewhere? I'd like to see those photos, if I could. And that drawing you talked about too. Something about that foot, the way you describe it—it sounds familiar to me, somehow. Like I've heard about it, or read about it, somewhere before."

"You too? I've had that feeling about it myself. I just haven't been able to figure out why yet."

"Well, maybe I can, given the chance. See if you can fax that stuff out to me tomorrow, huh?"

"I'll do it first thing in the morning," I said.

Then I promised her I'd be careful an even dozen times and hung up the phone.

• • •

Fifteen minutes later, Bad Dog and I were standing on the porch of our former hotel cabin, waiting for someone to answer the door. He hadn't liked it one bit, but I'd made Dozer Meadows stay behind at the trailer park with Joe. I felt imposing upon the cabin's new tenants to root around in their toilet tank was going to be hard enough to pull off without having a one-man death squad shadowing our every move. I was thinking at the time that we were going to have the hotel manager retrieve Dog's money for us, but the manager was out of his office when we got there and I didn't want to test Meadows's patience waiting for his return.

So it was just Dog and me standing there when the cabin door eventually opened and a squat, square-shouldered little man in a floral red kimono said, "Yes? What is it?"

There were a hundred different ways to answer that question, but I told him the truth. Flat out. I told him we were looking for jewelry and not cash, but other than that, I gave it to him straight. And he bought it. He asked us to wait a few minutes for his wife to come out of the bathroom; then he let us right in.

"Don't be embarrassed. I've got a couple of rugrats at home myself," he told me. "They do this kind of stupid stuff all the time."

I was afraid Dog might answer that, so I pushed him into the bathroom and shut the door behind him before he could get his mouth open. The little man in the lovely kimono only made it halfway through explaining things to his wife before Dog emerged again, patting his pockets and grinning at me victoriously.

"Well?" I asked him a few minutes later, when we'd said all our thank-yous and good-byes and were standing back out on the porch again.

"I got it."

"All of it?"

He pulled the roll out of his pocket and started to count it.

"Theodore, don't do that now. It's too dark to see what you're doing, and I'm freezing out here. We can do that back at the trailer."

It was one of those orders a child hears but chooses to treat like elevator Muzak. He shook me off and kept counting, breathing the numbers aloud as he did so. "Three-forty, three-sixty, three-eighty—"

"Come on, Theodore," a familiar voice implored, dripping with unmistakable venom. "Be a good boy and do what your mother tells you."

Dog and I looked up to see Ray and Phil, our two old friends in the newspaper business, standing just below us at the foot of the porch. They were still dressed like Brooks Brothers mannequins, only more so this time; complementing each man's ensemble was a tan, full-length woolen coat with brown leather accents, pieces so exquisite they nearly took my breath away.

As did the gun I immediately noticed Phil was holding in one hand.

"Please don't make a sound, Mrs. Loudermilk, or Phil here will be forced to kill you," Ray said. "And your son." He sounded like a tour guide at Disneyland: pleasant, rehearsed, and thoroughly artificial.

"We've been looking all over for you people," he continued. "We were afraid we'd missed our chance to talk to you again."

"Ray was in a panic. But I told him you'd show up again, sooner or later," Phil said. Only now did I notice that his gun had a silencer on it.

"You forgot your camera," Bad Dog said.

Ray's partner grinned and shrugged, as we'd seen him do before, and said what we expected he'd say: "It's in the shop."

"What do you want with us?" I asked, directing the question to Ray.

"For the moment, we want you to step this way and come along with us. Now."

"Where are we going?"

"Not far. Get a move on, Mrs. Loudermilk. We're in a hurry here, all right?"

There was nothing appealing about the thought of following these two anywhere, but Ray's brand of salesmanship had managed to convince me of one thing at least: He and Phil were prepared to kill us both if we didn't go along with the program.

"Let's do what the man says, Theodore," I told Dog.

We were led around the backside of the cabin to the rim of the Canyon itself, beyond the dark walking path and behind a small stand of trees. To get here, we'd had to pass by a few people still wandering about outdoors, a couple of young kids holding hands, and a pair of joggers running in opposite directions, but for the most part, we had gone undetected; every other visitor in the park seemed to realize that the Grand Canyon wasn't much to see at night, and had turned in accordingly. Phil had put the gun in one of his coat pockets, in any case, so that had anyone actually taken notice of us, they would have dismissed us as benign. Odd-looking perhaps, but benign.

So here we were, poor Dog and me: hidden from everyone's view, alone and unarmed, facing the least friendly end of a maniac's gun on the one hand, and a three-thousand-foot drop on the other.

Does that sound like a bad hair day to you, or what?

"Step farther back, if you would," Ray said, directing us to back up until the jagged edge of the Canyon was less than a yard behind us. "There. That's fine. Just fine."

"If it's the money you want, take it," Bad Dog said, holding his roll of bills forward for Ray to accept.

"Thanks, no. But that was a nice thought." He and Phil turned to each other and had a good laugh.

"Well, if you don't want money, what do you want?" I asked, starting to feel more angry than afraid. "You certainly aren't doing all this just to get a newspaper story."

"That, dear lady, is quite true," Ray said. "We're not after a story. And as you might guess, we never were. What we're after is information. Some simple answers to a few simple questions."

"Like what?"

"Like where is Filly Gee?" Phil jumped in.

"Who?"

"Filly Gee, Mrs. Loudermilk," Ray said, his voice getting a sharp, unexpected edge to it. "The man Mr.

Bettis told you about before he died. Remember?''

"I don't know what you're talking about. Mr. Bettis never told any of us anything. He was dead when we found him, we've told you that a thousand times.''

"He never mentioned the name Filly Gee to you? Or told you where he might be hiding?''

"No. We don't know any Philly Gees. Who or what is Philly Gee?''

"Just a man worth a lot of money to whoever helps us find him. Does that refresh your memory at all?''

"How much money are you talkin' about?'' Bad Dog asked.

I would have stuffed a bar of soap down his throat if I had had one.

"Oh, I don't know,'' Ray said, pretending to be mulling it over. "Say, fifteen grand?''

"You could offer us fifteen million, and it wouldn't make any difference,'' I said. "We don't know this Philly Gee of yours. We'd never even heard of him until this very minute.''

"He's got three toes, right?'' Bad Dog asked.

Ray gave Phil a brief glance, then turned back to Dog and nodded. "That's right.''

I suddenly wished my husband were here; nothing would have suited the moment better than a good "Jeez Looweez.''

"Then you do know him,'' Ray said.

"No. We don't,'' I cut in, slapping a hand over my son's open mouth.

"Mrs. Loudermilk, if the young man wants to talk, I think you should let him talk.''

"He doesn't know what he's saying! You dangled fifteen thousand dollars in front of him, so he said the first thing that came into his head. He was *guessing*."

"Guessing? He was guessing that the man we're looking for just happens to have three toes? Please, Mrs. Loudermilk. You're insulting my intelligence."

"Mine too," Phil said.

"Look. We saw a picture, that's all," I told them. "Of a foot with three toes. But we know absolutely nothing about who it belongs to."

"What kind of picture?" Ray asked, sounding very skeptical.

"It was a drawing. A sketch."

"Whose sketch? Who drew it?"

"We don't know, but . . . we suspect Mr. Bettis drew it."

"You suspect?"

It was a risky thing to do, but I told them everything. It seemed pretty clear to me that they were going to hear it all anyway, one way or another, so rather than oblige them one answer to one question at a time, I just filled them in all at once, barely pausing to take a breath. I figured that once they were made to understand how little we knew about Bettis and "Philly Gee," they'd let us go, and take their inquisitive little minds elsewhere.

But I figured wrong.

"What do you think, Phil?" Ray asked his partner when I'd told them all there was to tell.

"I think she's telling it straight. They can't help us."

"Yeah. That's what I think too."

"What about the pictures she talked about? Shouldn't we go get them?"

"Naw." Ray shook his head. "She says the house isn't there anymore, and I believe her. What are we going to do, drive down there to stare at an empty lot?" He turned to me. "I'm very sorry for all the trouble, Mrs. Loudermilk. But Phil and me, we had to be certain you weren't holding out on us. I hope you understand."

"Frankly, I don't," I said. "But then, I don't really want to. I just want to go back to my husband and forget this whole thing ever happened. Now, if you gentlemen will excuse us . . ."

I took Bad Dog's hand and started to walk away, but Phil stepped smoothly to one side to bar our way.

"I was afraid he was gonna do that," Bad Dog said.

"I wish I could trust you and your son to keep quiet about all this, Mrs. Loudermilk, because if I could, it would not be necessary to kill you," Ray said. "But I can't. I don't know either of you that well."

"Now wait a minute, man," Bad Dog said, his voice shaking.

"Again, my apologies. You're both victims of circumstance more than any anything else, but I feel responsible for you all the same. Rest assured I'll try to be a better judge of character in the future." He turned to Phil and said, "Make it quick."

Then he walked away.

Left alone to do the dirty work, Phil smiled at Dog and me and said, "Don't worry, folks. This isn't going to hurt a bit. I'm a professional."

With that, I closed my eyes and waited to die.

And waited.

And waited.

But nothing happened. The gun didn't go *pop,* the pain didn't come, my heart didn't slam to a stop. Time merely stood still, marred only by sound. The sound of some kind of struggle.

I opened my eyes again.

And there stood Dozer Meadows, pinning Phil to the trunk of a tree with one hand clamped tight over the smaller man's throat. Even in the dim moonlight, I could see Phil's eyes getting bigger and his face turning an unsettling shade of some undetermined color. The gun was still in his right hand, however, and he appeared to be fighting with everything he had to raise it from his side up to where Meadows's menacing face loomed.

"Put the gun down, man," Meadows advised him.

But Phil wouldn't listen.

"I'm warnin' you, man. Put the gun *down,* all right? Right now!"

Again Phil chose to ignore the order. The gun rose another fraction of an inch in his hand, and Meadows saw it.

Without another word, the big man lifted Phil over his head and tossed him into the Canyon. I felt something fly over my shoulder, and then I heard the screams.

I thought the echoes would never die.

____ 10 __

"Mrs. Loudermilk, my name is Alex Medavoy."

He was a handsome young man in a very bland way, tall but not thin, dark-haired and clean-shaven. Clean-shaven to the point of being glossy-cheeked, in fact. His dark blue suit fit, but did not excite; ditto for his crisp white shirt and burgundy tie. His cologne was wholly unmemorable.

He was an FBI man, he said. I would have never guessed.

We were sitting in Ranger Cooper's office, a by now all too familiar setting for me, but Cooper was not in the room with us. I'd been sitting here now for almost an hour, alone, expecting the ranger to come in and ask me all the questions that needed to be asked about the circumstances of Phil the cameraman's death, but in had walked Mr. Medavoy instead. He sat down in the chair beside me—not the one behind Cooper's desk, mind you, but the one right at my left elbow—showed me his ID, and then watched as I nearly lost my lunch all over his lap.

The Feds!

"You look pale. Should I get you some water?"

"No, no, no." I shook my head and took a deep breath. "I'm okay. It's just that . . . all this excitement . . ."

"Of course. You've been through quite a bit tonight. I understand. We'll try to make this as brief as possible, all right?"

I nodded and said, "Please."

He smiled. "Wonderful. We'll start with something simple. Mrs. Loudermilk, do you have any idea who the two men were who accosted you and your son this evening?"

"They said their names were Ray and Phil. They told us they were newspaper reporters."

"And you believed that?"

"No. I didn't."

"And why was that?"

"Because they didn't act like reporters. They didn't look like reporters. And they had guns and Instamatic cameras."

Medavoy raised an eyebrow. "Instamatic cameras? I don't understand."

I told him about the toy camera Phil had been carrying around when we first met him.

"Oh. I see," Medavoy said, grinning. "Then they never told you who they really were."

"No. Who were they?"

"Just a pair of hoods from back east. Musclemen out of St. Louis. Their real names aren't important. What is important is that you managed to make their acquaintance without getting badly hurt. Most of the people those two have bumped into over the years weren't that lucky, I'm afraid.''

"You mean they were hired killers? For the mob?''

"It'd be more accurate to say they were couriers, Mrs. Loudermilk. Capable of killing, yes, but that was not their area of expertise. I venture to say, you and your son Theodore would be dead by now if it had been. In all probability, Mr. Meadows as well.''

That water he had tried to offer me a moment earlier was starting to sound pretty good; my tongue was beginning to feel like that of a camel, an hour removed from safari.

"Where is Ray now?'' I asked, curious. The last time I'd seen him, he'd been sprawled out facedown on the walk path where Dozer Meadows had dropped him, looking a good deal like a fresh corpse waiting for the coroner's wagon to stop by.

"He's at the medical station here, getting patched up,'' Medavoy said. "Meadows broke his jaw in three places and moved his nose to a different spot on his face. He looks like hell, but I'm told he'll survive.''

"Thank God.'' I was, again, hearing Phil's terrified voice diminish into the Canyon. I wondered if I always would.

"You're pretty lucky the big man came along when he did,'' Medavoy said.

"Yes. We are.''

"I would have preferred to have Colletto—excuse me, Phil—alive too, but it sounds like he gave Meadows no choice but to do what he did to him.''

I recognized this as a question, not a comment, so I said, "That's true. Phil wouldn't put down the gun, so . . ." I was unable to finish the sentence.

"I understand. It was self-defense."

"Yes."

Medavoy nodded his head, satisfied. "Well. Enough of that. Let's push on, shall we?"

I waited for him to do so.

"Good. Let's talk about the kind of questions Ray and Phil asked you. All right? Tell me what they said they wanted to know, exactly."

"They wanted to know if Mr. Bettis had told us anything about somebody named Philly Gee before he died. They seemed to be interested in finding out where this Philly Gee person, whoever he is, was hiding. That's what they said, 'hiding.' "

"And did you tell them?"

"What?"

"Did you tell them where this Filly Gee was hiding?"

"No." I was confused by the question. "We don't *know* any Philly Gee. Who in the world is Philly Gee?"

"Then Mr. Bettis really was dead when you found him. He never actually spoke to you, about Filly Gee, about anything."

"No. He was dead. Conversation between the living and the dead is very minimal, Mr. Medavoy. That's because dead people don't do much talking, and they don't listen very well either. They're a lot like policemen, in that respect."

"I'm sorry if this is overly familiar territory for you, Mrs. Loudermilk, but these questions have to be asked."

I just answered his apology with silence.

"Did either Ray or Phil admit to killing Mr. Bettis in your trailer?"

"No."

"Did they ever ask you if you knew who might have killed him?"

"Not that I recall. Didn't the man they have in jail down in Flagstaff kill Mr. Bettis?"

"If you don't mind, Mrs. Loudermilk, we'll leave all the questions for me to ask, okay?"

"I'm sorry. I just wondered—"

"While we're on the subject of Flagstaff—why did you and your family drive down there this morning?"

"To pick up our trailer from the sheriff's station. They had taken her down there to run some lab tests on her, and when they said we could have her back, we decided to go down and get her ourselves. Why?"

"And that's all you did while you were down there? Pick up your trailer from the sheriff's station?"

"Well . . ."

I could tell from the look on his face that he already knew the answer to his question. And as if to prove it, he opened the manila envelope he'd been holding in his lap and handed me a set of eight-by-ten black-and-white photographs.

"These were taken in Flagstaff this afternoon, Mrs. Loudermilk. Maybe you can tell me what they mean."

They were all candid shots of Joe, Dog, and me, first at Geoffry Bettis's home, then up at the vacant lot that had been 505 West Fir, where we were joined in a couple of shots by Dozer Meadows. In other words, it was a virtual exposé of three amateur detectives caught in the act of butting in where they don't belong. It was embarrassing, to say the least. So this, I thought to myself, was what Bad Dog always meant when his father and I would get the goods on him and he'd mumble two words dejectedly under his breath:

Stone busted.

Needless to say, I came clean again. What else could I do? Dog wasn't here to show me how to lie effectively, and I was getting a little too good at that for my tastes, anyway, so I went with the honest approach. They always say on TV that if you cooperate with the authorities, they'll go easy on you. Of course, they also say Listerine kills the germs that cause bad breath.

Medavoy remained unnervingly quiet after I had stopped talking. I tried to read his eyes for some clue to my fate, but he kept them turned away from me. Deliberately, I thought.

"Am I in trouble?" I asked him when I couldn't take his silence any longer.

"That all depends," he said, sounding grim.

"On what?"

"On whether or not you've told me everything. If you've been holding anything back, if you've neglected to tell me anything at all—"

"I haven't. I've told you everything I know, believe me."

He got quiet again, but this time he made a point of allowing me to see his eyes. "You really don't know who Filly Gee is?"

"No. I really don't." I shook my head until I thought it was going to fly off.

"And you'd never seen the man in Bettis's photographs before? Here in the park, or anywhere else?"

"No. Never."

"What about your husband, or your son Theodore? Could they have recognized him, do you think?"

"No. They'd never seen him before either. He was a stranger to all of us, I'm certain of it."

Medavoy sighed, slapped his thigh, and said, "All right then, Mrs. Loudermilk. In that case, I only have one more question for you. Think you can handle that?" He smiled his J. Edgar Hoover/game show host smile at me again.

"Sure. I don't see why not."

He pulled another eight-by-ten from his envelope and handed it to me. "Tell me. Have you ever seen this woman before? Around the park here, or maybe even down in Flagstaff somewhere?"

She was stepping into the back seat of a taxi. She wore a white cotton dress cut well above the knee, form-fitting and designed for show, and a matching, large-brimmed white hat that washed her face in deep shadow. A mane of what appeared to be golden-yellow hair spilled out of the hat and fell softly to her shoulders; you could almost smell the sweet scent of soap in it, it looked so clean and well kept.

I'd never seen the lady before, and I told Medavoy so.

"Who is she? Mrs. Philly Gee?" I asked him.

He took all the photographs from my hands and said, "You might call her that." He seemed to want to say more, but he didn't.

That was just fine by me.

"Well, that's it," he said simply. "If I can think of any more questions to ask you later, Mrs. Loudermilk, I'll see you in the morning out at the trailer park before you leave. Otherwise, this is good-bye. And thank you." He reached out and shook my hand; then he walked me to the door.

"You aren't going to tell me what this was all about?" I asked, more than a little naively.

"No ma'am. It'd be best for all concerned if I didn't. You'll just have to trust me on that."

"But if Ray and Phil were really the ones who killed Mr. Bettis—"

"I never suggested that they were. I merely asked you if they ever implicated themselves in Mr. Bettis's murder, and you assured me that they did not."

"Yes, but—"

"Mrs. Loudermilk. Please. Everything is under control here, I promise you. So relax."

He put his hand on my shoulder with one hand and opened the door with the other. I was tempted to hold my ground just to illustrate how little I cared for being treated so condescendingly, but I knew there'd be no point. He had told me all he was going to, and nothing was going to change that.

"All right, Mr. Medavoy," I said. "I guess I'll just have to trust you, as you say."

"Yes ma'am."

"But do me a favor, will you? Please don't come looking for me in the morning. As tired as I am right now, I plan to sleep in until noon tomorrow, at least. You want to talk to me, come by anytime after one. I should be fine by then."

I laughed, but Medavoy let me do it all by myself.

"I'm afraid you misunderstand. You'll be leaving in the morning, as I said. Bright and early."

"Excuse me?"

"What I'm trying to say here, Mrs. Loudermilk, is that if you and your family aren't off the park grounds by nine-thirty tomorrow morning, I'll have you arrested and charged with obstruction of justice. Among other things. Do you get my meaning, ma'am?"

The smile on his face now was not the same one he'd shown me earlier. This one had teeth in it. The sharp, serrated kind of teeth great white sharks like to use to slit open their prey before devouring the intestines in one bite.

I told the FBI man I got his meaning, and made fast tracks for Lucille.

"I don't like this," I said, one more time.

I wasn't keeping count, but Bad Dog apparently was. "You've said that a hundred times, Moms. 'I don't like this.' 'I don't like this.' 'I don't like this.' Man, change the recording already, please."

"That's 'record,' " Big Joe said.

"What?"

"The expression is 'change the *record.*' Not 'the recording.' "

"Oh. Like in 'world record,' huh?"

"No. Like in 'broken record.' A musical record, a forty-five or an LP."

"Ah, I gotcha."

"Only this record's got a scratch on it, so the needle's always jumpin' backward and playin' the same thing over an' over again. 'I don't like this, *brippp,* I don't like this, *brippp,* I don't like this, *brippp*—' "

"All right, all right," I said, bouncing a palm off the side of my husband's head. "I get the point. You want me to shut up, I'll shut up." I gave them both a chance to actually say it—*Shut up*—but neither man took the bait. "But I don't like what we're doing here, and neither do you. It just doesn't feel right."

We were on our way to Texas. We'd been driving south along Interstate 17 for about an hour now, after having seen Dog's playmate Dozer Meadows off at the Grand Canyon airport on our way out of the park. Meadows intended to use the money we'd given him to fly out to Pittsburgh in time for the Steelers game tomorrow afternoon. He still wasn't going to be able to play, he said, but he missed the team too much to just watch the game on TV from his home back in Los Angeles. He told us he was going to walk the sidelines down on the field and, depending on how the Raiders were doing, kick ass where and when it needed to be kicked.

"Later, Mrs. Loudermilk," he had said at the boarding gate, smothering me in a bear hug big enough to warm the state of Montana. I could have dozed off in there, it felt so good.

The big man was worried about me. He was afraid he

had scarred me for life dispatching Phil the way he had before my horrified eyes, but I told him he was just being silly. After all, if he had not come looking for Dog and me when he did, having grown impatient waiting for our return to the trailer park with his money, it would have very likely been *our* bodies the authorities were endeavoring to raise from the dry Canyon floor this day, and not Phil's. Meadows had done the only thing he could do under the circumstances, I promised him, and there was no need to worry about me; I was just fine.

I think he believed the first part, but would always doubt the last, no matter what I said.

Dog, meanwhile, wanted to go with him, of course, but Joe said he was going to have to go folded up inside a Samsonite bag if he did, because his father and I were too tapped out to buy him a ticket. We ended up agreeing to take him along with us to Texas, and from there we'd fly him to the destination of his choice once his sister Mo had wired us some fresh cash.

Alex Medavoy hadn't shown up to see it, but we had fled the Canyon's trailer park at eight sharp, well within our nine-thirty deadline. It had been a hard thing for me to do, run for high ground like a mouse catching sight of a cat, just because a government man snapped his fingers, but Joe, surprisingly, had taken the insult far worse than I. He had been ready to leave for three days now, so much so that I thought he might even appreciate Agent Medavoy's assistance in finally persuading me to go, but no. Joe had become incensed instead. Why I hadn't fully expected this reaction, I don't know; the best way to light a fire under Joe has always been to try and tell him what is and is not his business. Especially when the person doing the telling is a badge-flashing government stooge.

Still, we tucked our tails beneath us and obeyed orders, on time and without complaint. In less than seven days, we had dodged more bullets than the Allied forces had at Normandy, and we knew we'd be pressing our luck to remain sitting targets at the Canyon for so much as one more day. Leaving the park now, under duress, would exact a certain cost in terms of wounded pride and unsatisfied curiosity, yes, but we could live with these annoyances, given time. The same could not be said for a five-year stretch in the Gulag, courtesy of the Federal Bureau of Investigation. Hard time and old convicts don't mix all that well.

Putting something behind you and putting it out of your mind, however, are not always the same thing. Try as I might to think about something else, I just couldn't shake the feeling that our fleeing the Canyon at the FBI's request was leaving the door open for something terrible to happen. That they had sent us packing to cover up something they did not want widely known was obvious; what was not were the possible consequences of letting them have their way. And that was the doubt that nagged at me: Who was going to pay for the damage control job we were helping the Bureau pull off at the Grand Canyon, and at what price?

A human life, perhaps?

It was a question worth worrying about, as far as I was concerned, and so worry I did, as our exile to Texas came closer and closer to reality with each passing mile marker. "I don't like this," I kept saying, over and over again, until Dog and Joe had finally been forced to voice their sarcastic objections. Eventually, I found the willpower to stop saying the words—but I never could make the thought itself go away.

We made our first stop for gas in Black Canyon City, Arizona, a few minutes past ten in the morning, and while Joe worked the pumps and Dog used the men's room, I found a pay phone and called Mo. I had promised her the night before that I would fax her the photos and line drawing her brother had removed from Geoffry Bettis's safety deposit box on Thursday, but these items were no longer mine to fax; Medavoy had confiscated them. As it happened, that was just as well, though, for once Mo heard me say "FBI," she lost all interest in the photos and drawing, or anything else pertaining to the late Mr. Bettis.

"Mother, just hang up the phone and start driving again," she said when I'd brought her up-to-date on the latest events of our Grand Canyon adventure. "Get the heck out of Arizona, and don't ever look back."

"Mo, you're acting silly," I said.

"No I'm not. I'm being smart. You don't mess around with the FBI, Mom. The FBI squashed Al Capone—they wouldn't think twice about squashing the likes of you. Now, I don't know what they have to do with what happened to you and Daddy at the Grand Canyon, and I don't care. All I know is, they let you go in one piece, and I want you both to stay that way. Understand?"

"I understand perfectly. You don't want us to get hurt."

"That's right. I don't."

"But you don't mind if someone else does."

"Mother, please."

"They're trying to hide something, Mo, and I think we both know what it is. Don't we?"

"Mother—"

"That man the Coconino County Sheriff's Department has in jail back in Flagstaff didn't kill Geoffry Bettis, Mo. Somebody else did. And whoever that somebody else is, the FBI is going out of their way to protect them. Even if it means an innocent man has to go to prison for a crime he didn't commit."

"Mother, for God's sake! You were almost killed by two Mafia hit men last night!"

"They weren't hit men. They were couriers," I said.

"Fine. They were couriers. With guns. Who nearly showed you and Bad Dog the fastest way down to the bottom of the Grand Canyon!"

She said it as if I needed to be reminded.

"Mother, listen to me. Please. Whatever's going on up there, you don't want any part of it. If you even think about interfering, they'll stop you, one way or another. They'll either throw you in jail, as promised, or use somebody you care about as leverage to keep you in line. And nobody—least of all me—would be able to stop them from doing it. Believe me when I tell you that. Now—is that what you want? Really?"

I didn't say anything.

"Well?"

"Of course that's not what I want. But—"

"No buts, Mother. I don't want to hear any buts. All I want to hear you say is that you understand what I'm telling you completely, and that you and Daddy are going to go on ahead to Texas as planned and forget all about the Grand Canyon. Aren't you?"

Again, I fell silent.

"I want to hear you say it, Mother," Mo said sternly.

I told her we were going to continue on to Texas and forget all about the Grand Canyon.

"Thank you," she said, her voice filled with relief.

"We're going to need you to wire some money ahead to San Antonio," I said, changing the subject before she could get around to questioning my sincerity.

"Fine. How much?"

"About eight hundred should do it."

"Eight hundred? Isn't that a little—" She stopped herself, struck by a sudden thought. "Oh. I forgot. You've got the human debt machine with you, don't you?"

"Mo, don't start. I'm not in any mood."

"I've never seen anything like him. He can take fresh cash and turn it into confetti in less time than it takes the average man or woman to inhale. And still you and Daddy keep right on bankrolling him."

"We're not bankrolling him. We're just . . . helping him find his way."

"His way *where?* To the poorhouse? The boy is jinxed, Mother. He couldn't make an honest dollar from a deal if he were the last rice salesman in China. All he ever does with all the ammo you two give him is shoot himself in the foot.''

''That's enough, Mo. I don't want to hear any more.''

''I know you don't. But as the one you and Daddy turn to every time one of that knothead's 'investments' turns sour—''

''You feel it's your duty to advise us against giving him any more money. Of course. Little girl, I understand what you're saying, and I agree with you completely. That's why we're not giving him anything this time but his airfare home. Or didn't I mention that?''

Now Mo was the one not talking.

''No, I guess I didn't. You never gave me a chance to, did you?''

She maintained her stubborn silence a full moment longer, then said, ''I guess you think I owe you an apology now, huh?''

''You guess right. You *do* owe me an apology. Your father, too.''

''I'm sorry. I overreacted.''

''Yes. You did.''

I let her feel uncomfortable for another minute or so before warming up to say good-bye.

When we had taken to the road again, I spent the next forty-five minutes poring over the latest issue of *People* magazine. A nine-year-old boy who had swallowed his mother's diaphragm and lived to tell about it was on the cover. The caption was a quote, something the child had said to explain himself that the media had by now made famous: "I THOUGHT IT WAS A DONUT!"

Reading the overly homogenized news stories that *People* passed off as journalism had long been a guilty pleasure of mine. It was like being a tabloid junkie without having to deal with the inferiority complex. You could indulge in all the sensationalism and not feel like a total idiot doing it. No Martians or miracle cures for heartburn; no pregnant six-year-olds or Big Foot sightings at Kmart. It was always just Hollywood marriages on the rocks, unruly television teen throbs on the loose, and the exploits and capture of the Criminal of the Month. With pictures.

For instance, this latest issue of the magazine featured a story about a multiracial lesbian couple who were trying to adopt an adorable pair of Korean twins in Colorado, where the law firmly frowns upon such things. I was three paragraphs into the article, and we were two hundred miles out of Flagstaff, when—

It hit me.

"Joe, pull over," I said.

"What?"

"I said, pull over. At the next exit with a gas station, pull over and stop!"

"For what? We just stopped for gas!"

"We're not stopping to get gas. We're stopping so I can find a *phone*."

"Dottie, you just got through using the phone, too. Now, what in the hell—"

"You miss this turnoff, Joe Loudermilk, and I'm gonna have your behind!"

He only had about eight seconds to make the turn, but he made it with room to spare.

The first thing Mo said when she realized it was me was: "Danny Gottifucci."

"Yes! Yes!" I said. "When—"

"About three minutes after I hung up the phone. I guess it must have struck you roughly around the same time."

"No. It was more like five minutes ago, for me. I was looking through the latest copy of *People* magazine, when something you said—"

"About Bad Dog always shooting himself in the foot."

"Yes. When that made me remember the story they did on Danny Gottifucci a few years ago. The mob informant who'd lost part of his right foot when his friends and family just barely missed having him killed."

Gottifucci hadn't been seen or heard from since. He had been a midlevel crime boss somewhere out on the East Coast who had placed himself at the mercy of the Justice Department by making one simple mistake: He had done some of his own killing. Murdering an old mistress who had belittled his virility in public had given him no out from a date with the state executioner other than to rat on his friends, so he had done just that— reluctantly so before the failed attempt on his life, not so reluctantly afterward. Then he had disappeared. One more satisfied customer of the FBI's vaunted witness protection program.

"You think Gottifucci is your Philly Gee?" Mo asked

me, sounding like she already knew the answer.

"I don't know. Was Gottifucci from Philadelphia?"

"It could have been Philadelphia. I'm not sure. But I seem to recall it was Baltimore."

"Then you *don't* think he's Philly Gee."

"On the contrary. I think that makes a lot of sense. It certainly would seem to explain a few things, anyway. Like why both the FBI and the mob are so interested in his whereabouts. And the house, of course."

"The house?"

"Yes. The house. The one you said was missing."

"Oh."

"I mean, if that's where Gottifucci has been living all this time, and someone like Geoffry Bettis found out about it—"

"The FBI would get him out of town and try to cover up their tracks afterward."

"Yes."

"So Mr. Bettis was trying to blackmail Gottifucci."

"That's what it sounds like to me. You said Bettis was always on the lookout for a fast buck, and that his room was full of true-crime magazines and stuff. If he'd spotted Gottifucci on the street one day, depending on how much Gottifucci's changed over the years, it isn't too hard to imagine Bettis recognizing him. Is it?"

"No. But if all he did was spot him on the street—"

"How would he know what Gottifucci's foot looked like?"

"Yes."

"Simple. He could have seen a picture of it in one of his magazines, or something."

I thought about that for a moment. "Okay. Let's say he did. Assuming the things we found in his safety deposit box were what he was going to threaten Gottifucci with, what was a drawing of his own supposed to prove? The photos were hard evidence of Gottifucci's presence in Flagstaff, all right, but if anyone with the same magazine could have described the appearance of Gottifucci's foot . . ."

"Yes, yes, I see your point. Why bother with the drawing? He couldn't have expected it to have any real impact on Gottifucci, unless the exact appearance of Gottifucci's foot was something a person could know about only after seeing it in the flesh, with their own eyes."

"Exactly. And as Mr. Bettis was a shoe salesman—"

"He very well could have done that. Providing he had once been lucky enough to have Gottifucci for a customer, anyway."

"Pops said to get off the phone and come on," Bad Dog suddenly said. I turned around and there he was, chewing on a Mars bar. Beyond him, through the service station's dingy windows, I could see his father propped up against our truck's front fender, arms crossed and blood boiling as he returned my stare.

"I've got to go, Mo," I told my daughter. "Your father's having a fit."

"Go where, Mother? What are you going to do?"

"I don't know yet. But I'll think of something."

"Mother, put Daddy on the phone. I want to talk to Daddy."

"We have to go, Mo. I'll call you later."

"Mother, don't you dare even think about going back there, you hear me? Don't you dare even *think* about it!"

"I love you, too, baby. Kiss my grandchildren for me."

I hung up the phone.

"You better hurry it up. Pops is pretty pissed," Dog said, showing me the way out.

I told him he hadn't seen anything yet.

As I expected, Big Joe let me walk two miles up the interstate with my thumb in the air before it sank into his thick skull that I was going to return to Flagstaff, with or without him and Dog. He'd turned a deaf ear on everything Mo and I had deduced and told me if I wanted to travel north instead of south, I'd have to do it on foot, because he wasn't going to drive me. So I'd promptly stepped out of the truck and started walking. North.

I thought he might try to pull a fast one—wait until I was back in the cab again, then make a quick U-turn and floor it for Texas—but he didn't. Mad as he was, he knew better. I'd only been mildly tempted to go back to Flagstaff before, when a *feeling* that something was amiss there was all I really had eating at me, but now that I had a theory to go along with my suspicions, nothing was going to stop me from going back there to prove it out. Nothing. If the car thief and armed robber they were holding in the Flagstaff jail had not killed Geoffry

Bettis, his only hope of ever being cleared of the crime was me.

The trouble was, I didn't have a clue as to how to go about it.

Imagine my surprise, then, when Big Joe did, and actually went so far out of his way as to say so.

"We've got to go back to the Coconino County Sheriff's Department and tell them what we know," he said. "If we can convince them we're telling the truth, their hatred for the Feds alone will persuade them to reopen the case. Nothing gets a cop hotter than the idea that he's been used, in one fashion or another, to do the Feds' dirty work."

I couldn't help but grin. Finally, it had happened: the long-awaited reemergence of Inspector Joe Loudermilk II of Scotland Yard.

"So how do we convince them we're telling the truth?" I asked.

"I don't know. But I have an idea," Big Joe said.

And he did.

____ 11 __

"Is this what you wanted?" Geoffry Bettis's widow asked.

She tossed a thick manila folder on our table and sat down. The late afternoon lunch crowd at our favorite restaurant in Flagstaff, Perkins, was light, so our waitress appeared almost immediately to ask if our new guest needed to see a menu. Mrs. Bettis said she didn't.

I reached for the folder before Joe could and began to leaf through it. Sure enough, just as we'd hoped when we called Mrs. Bettis two hours ago, it was a poor man's dossier on Danny Gottifucci: news clippings, photographs, the works. No illustrations of Gottifucci's three-toed right foot, though. And no mention of the nickname "Philly Gee," either.

"Well?" Mrs. Bettis asked me.

"This is it, all right. The Danny Gottifucci file. You found this in your husband's room?"

"Yes." She nodded her head.

Joe took the folder from me to look it over himself. Bad Dog kept right on shoveling chili into his mouth and ignoring everything else.

"What does it mean?" Mrs. Bettis asked. Unlike the

last time we had seen her, today she sounded like she had a genuine interest in what we had to say.

"It means we're at least half right," Joe said, more to me than to her. "Your husband did know about Danny Gottifucci."

"Who is Danny Gottifucci?"

We told her the mobster's story and much of our own in abbreviated terms.

"We think your husband waited on Gottifucci at the shoe store where he worked, got one look at the three toes on his right foot, and recognized him," Joe said. "Then, knowing he was in hiding from the mob—"

"He tried to blackmail Gottifucci."

"Yes. Our guess is, he followed Gottifucci out of the store the day he came in, found out where he lived, and then came back later to take some pictures of him around the house."

"And once he had the pictures, we think he set up a meeting with Gottifucci for last Tuesday at the Canyon. Only something went wrong," I continued. "Either Gottifucci double-crossed him, the mob tried to squeeze him, or the FBI stepped in to protect Gottifucci. Whichever of the three it was, your husband ended up dead."

"And Gottifucci?" Mrs. Bettis asked. "What happened to him?"

"His friends the Feds have probably already got him set up in a new home somewhere," Joe said. "On the other side of the continent, most likely."

Mrs. Bettis made herself some time to think by lighting up a cigarette. I'd been wondering what had happened to her smoking habit. Fanning a match in the air to put out its flame, she said, "You say the mob was up at the Canyon looking for Gottifucci?"

I nodded.

"How did they know he was up there?"

I looked at Joe, and he looked at me. It was a question we hadn't given much thought to before now.

"We don't know," I said finally.

"But it isn't really too surprising, them finding out about it," Joe said. "They've got ears everywhere. Everything the Feds know, they know, eventually."

Mrs. Bettis nodded slowly and blew a stream of smoke over her left shoulder, apparently content with Joe's explanation. "So where do you Sherlocks go now?"

"Back to the Sheriff's Department," I said. "We're hoping once they see this"—I gestured with the file she'd brought us—"they'll admit their investigation into your husband's murder is worth reopening. What happens after that is out of our hands."

She just nodded her head again.

"You're free to come with us, if you like," Joe said. "The more the merrier, I always say."

Mrs. Bettis smiled. "Thanks, but I'll pass," she said, getting to her feet. She stood there looking at the three of us for a long time. "You people are okay. Nosy as hell, but okay."

"Thank you," I said.

"But you should know one thing before you go see the Sheriff's Department."

"Yes?"

"Well, it couldn't have happened exactly the way you

described it. How Geoff found out about Gottifucci, I mean. You said Geoff must have sold him a pair of shoes at the store, and that's how he saw his foot. Right?''

"That's what we suspect happened, yeah," Joe said.

"Well, I don't think it happened that way. It couldn't have."

"Why not?"

"Because Geoff didn't sell men's shoes. He sold ladies' shoes. That's the only kind of shoes his store sells." She stubbed her cigarette out in the ashtray at our table and said, "Just thought you might like to know."

She turned around and walked out.

Twenty minutes later, we were pulling into the visitors' parking lot of the Coconino County sheriff's station in Flagstaff. Learning that Geoffry Bettis had sold shoes to women and not to men had thrown us off stride for a moment, but not to the point that we ever considered changing our plans. It had been so nice and neat, the idea that Bettis could have stumbled onto Gottifucci in his capacity as a shoe salesman, but that didn't mean it had to have happened that way. Judging from the newspaper photographs in the file Mrs. Bettis had given us, Gottifucci hadn't changed much in the four years since his disappearance; the man in the photos Bettis had taken was a little slimmer and his hair loss more advanced, but other than that, he looked about the same. Had Bettis bumped into him on the street, there was no reason to believe he wouldn't have been able to recognize him, with or without his shoes on.

That was the line we were going to hand our old friends Detective Crowe and Detective Bollinger in a few minutes, anyway. And if it flew, great. If it didn't . . . we'd start for Texas again, this time with a clear conscience.

As usual, we ended up parking our truck and trailer in a far corner of the lot, where multiple spaces were readily available. The three of us stepped out of the Ford's cab and just stood there for a minute, exchanging nervous glances.

"You sure you want to do this?" Big Joe asked me.

I shook my head. "No. But we're going to do it anyway."

He nodded his head and we started walking.

We were moving past a big silver, four-door Oldsmobile when someone working under the hood said, "Pardon me. You wouldn't happen to have a set of jumper cables on you, would you?"

Joe saw the woman first; he was closest to the car. She was a moderately attractive brunette in a perfectly tailored gray business suit, with long legs and a ready smile. There was a light hint of rouge on her cheeks and the mere suggestion of blue eyeshadow on her eyelids. If I had kept my eyes on her face, I would have never thought twice about her, but her legs caught my attention and wouldn't let go. By the time I figured out where I had seen them before, it was too late: Joe was already standing beside her, ever the Good Samaritan, scanning the Olds's engine compartment for the source of her trouble.

"Joe, get away from there," I said, trying to be calm about it.

He turned toward me, confused by the order, until she made him aware of the gun in her hand by firmly poking him in the ribs with its nose.

"Anybody makes a sound, you all die," she said. "Anybody makes any sudden moves, same result. Do we understand each other?"

"Who—" Joe started to ask.

"No questions. No pregnant pauses. Just blind obedience, starting now. What do you say?" She poked Joe in the ribs with the gun again, hard. Bad Dog looked like he was about to speak, but I cut him a glance that instantly removed the thought from his mind. Satisfied that she had won our full cooperation, the brunette said, "All right. Back to your truck, everybody. *Slowly.*"

And that's what we did. We went back to our truck. Slowly.

"I knew you'd come back," Danny Gottifucci said.

If the photos Geoffry Bettis had taken of him were any indication, he hadn't been particularly handsome as a man, but as a woman he was really a looker. He knew how to dress, how to style a mean wig, and of course, as I've mentioned before, he had the kind of legs most chorus girls would die for. From a distance, you'd never know his secret; up close, you'd almost have to already have your suspicions about him to catch on. He looked that good.

"Our friend Alex Medavoy tried to tell me that he'd scared you off, that you were gone for good and would no longer pose a problem, but I told him he was crazy. I've been watching you, Mrs. Loudermilk, and you're a real bloodhound. Once you get the scent of something, you don't let go, do you?'' He laughed.

We were sitting in the cab of our Ford pickup; I was doing the driving and he was watching me do it. We were alone. Big Joe and Bad Dog were behind us inside Lucille, where they'd been told to stay put, keep quiet, and leave the trailer's windows alone if they ever wanted to see me alive again. We'd been on the road now for well over a half hour, once again heading south along Interstate 17, and had heard not a peep yet out of either Joe or Dog. Given Gottifucci's threat, I didn't expect that we ever would.

''You were the one watching me at Hopi House,'' I said, suddenly able to picture him, in drag, emerging from the curio shop amid a group of five other people.

Gottifucci nodded. ''It's like I've been saying. You're the curious type,'' he said, no longer finding it necessary to feminize his voice. ''I recognized that about you right away. That's why I've been so good about keeping an eye on you. There's no telling what a snoop like you will do, given the chance to screw up somebody else's business.''

''How did you know we'd turn up at the sheriff's station?''

''I didn't. But it seemed like a safe bet. Where else were you gonna go?''

I was having a hard time remembering to keep my eyes on the road, and not on the gun in his hand. ''Are you Philly Gee?'' I asked.

''Some people call me that. Yeah.'' He didn't seem to enjoy having to admit it.

''But you're not from Philly. You're supposed to be from Baltimore.''

''What? What does that have to do—'' I had opened my mouth to explain, when he started laughing again, catching on. ''Oh. I get it,'' he said. ''Philadelphia. You think Filly's short for Philadelphia.''

''Isn't it?''

''I'm afraid not. The name's F-I-L-L-Y, Mrs. L. Filly. Like the horse, not the city.''

''*Filly?*''

''That's right. Filly. A female horse. A sleazebag by the name of Sammy Slowhand gave me that name. The bookie. He thought it was cute, said he gave it to me on account of how much I always loved to play the ponies, but I knew better. Somehow, he'd found out about my— my *hobby,* shall we say?—and thought giving me that nickname might earn him a few laughs around the track.'' He shrugged and smiled. ''He never got the laughs, but he did get a nice funeral. You should've seen all the beautiful flowers.''

''You killed him?''

Gottifucci nodded.

''Just like you killed Geoffry Bettis.''

''More or less. Sammy was actually taken out by some friends of mine. Bettis, I did myself.''

''Why?''

''Come on, Mrs. Loudermilk. You know why. Because the little puke was trying to blackmail me, that's why. I'd gone into the store where he worked one day and bought some shoes from the son of a bitch, and he recognized me. Can you believe it? The son of a bitch recognized me!''

"He saw your foot," I said.

"Yeah. My foot. You know about that, huh?" As he had been doing every few minutes or so, he glanced at the sideview mirror on his side of the truck, making sure Big Joe and Bad Dog were behaving themselves inside Lucille. "Well, what can I tell you? I made a mistake. Leaving the house and going into town to shop for shoes was stupid enough, but letting some wise guy salesman like Bettis actually *fit* me was downright moronic. I was wearing stockings, sure, but he could see the outline of my toes right through 'em. Anybody could have." He sighed and then smiled again. "But you know how it is. When a girl needs shoes, she needs shoes."

The look on my face must have asked my next question for me, because he said, "I'm a cross-dresser, Mrs. Loudermilk. Not a transvestite. That means I'm really only in it for the clothes." He cracked up at his own joke. "At least, that's what my shrink used to tell me. The hack. I only bother with the wig and the makeup when I have to go out." His eyes drifted over to the highway ahead of us and he said, "Okay. Let's be very careful here, Mrs. L. We wouldn't want to do anything foolish, would we?"

The northbound Arizona state trooper cruised right by us, and I did nothing to stop him.

"Good girl," Gottifucci said, eyeing the sideview mirror outside his window again. "Now, if your son and your husband are as smart as you are . . ." He waited before going on. I peered into the mirror on my side and watched with him as the state trooper's taillights vanished over the horizon, having never slowed for a minute.

"Wonderful," Gottifucci said, blowing a strand of brown hair from in front of his eyes. "Now. As I was saying. This little . . . *problem* of mine. You'd never know it to see me now, I suppose, but the truth is, it's not that big a deal, really. That is, I hardly ever feel the need to dress up like this. Two or three times a year, that's the most I've ever really done it. That's why I was always able to keep it a secret. Other than that stupid nickname Sammy Slowhand gave me, there was never a word of talk about me being a cross-dresser from anybody, in or out of the family. Not a word.

"Still, even getting your rocks off only two or three lousy times a year can be difficult to pull off when the goddamn Feds are watching you like a hawk, keeping you on a leash like a fucking dog or something. They didn't care about my needs, all they cared about was keeping me alive. They pretended to understand, sure, but they really didn't. It was all a big joke to them, just like it was to Sammy."

He was getting angry, and that worried me. "The FBI didn't provide you with . . . what you needed?" I asked awkwardly, hoping to sound sympathetic.

"You mean clothes? Oh, sure they did. I got lots of clothes. Blouses and skirts, dresses and panty hose, bras, panties, nightgowns, and slips—the works. And shoes. Plenty of shoes."

"Then what—"

"What was the problem? Think about it for a minute, Mrs. Loudermilk. You're a woman. It'll come to you."

I didn't have the slightest idea what he was talking about, until I put myself in his place and asked myself how it would feel to have others buying my clothes for me, sight unseen.

"They didn't bring you anything you wanted to wear," I said.

"Exactly! You hit the nail right on the head," Gottifucci said. "What a man—or a woman—chooses to wear on his or her body is a very personal thing, Mrs. Loudermilk. You know that. What's acceptable to one individual may be unacceptable to another. The things the Feds were buying me were nice, sure, but they weren't *me*. And if they weren't *me*"—he shrugged— "they didn't make me feel good. And let's face it—the whole point of getting dressed is to feel good, isn't it?"

I would have agreed with him, except that our conversation and the images that were beginning to form in my head were starting to make me nauseous.

"So you see, it was only natural that I'd be tempted from time to time to go out and do my own shopping. Right? It was like an itch I had to scratch. Only I should've been more careful about it. I can see that now, of course. I should've just gone into that store, picked out a pair of shoes that appealed to me, and bought a pair my size. Period. No trying 'em on, no strolling before the mirror, just hand over the money, take the box, and get the hell out of there. That's what I should've done."

"But you didn't."

"No. I didn't. I made a careless play instead, and let

a two-bit loser like Bettis get his hooks into me, but good. I open my mail one day, and I find these photographs he's taken of me at the house. He says he knows who I am, and why I'm in Flagstaff. He says if two hundred thousand dollars isn't in his hands within three days, the people who've been looking for me are gonna get a phone call. Along with some pictures of their own.

"Right away, I know who it is trying to fleece me—the timing of this shit appearing in my mailbox and my trip into town is too coincidental, right? So what do you think I do to get this jerk off my back? Go back down to that shoe store and finish him myself? No. That's what I should've done, but that's not what I did. What I did instead, like an idiot, was ask Agent Medavoy to handle it. And naturally, being the worthless, spineless, *brain*less Fed that he is, he botched the job completely. *Completely.*

"He has his boys try and take Bettis out, and they miss. They *miss*. Medavoy says they were all set to blow him away in a phony liquor store robbery when a local cop breaks it up. But don't worry, Danny, he says, we'll try again. Only they never got the chance, because Bettis doesn't believe in coincidence any more than I do. He comes out of that liquor store smelling a rat, and immediately goes into a little hiding of his own. That's when I decided to disappear too."

He glanced at the road ahead, then went on. "The way I looked at it, if that was the best Agent Medavoy and his merry men could do to protect me, I was better off on my own. So I packed up and took off on 'em, to see if I could find Bettis myself."

"Then the FBI was looking for both of you," I said.

Gottifucci grinned. "Yeah. Bettis they eventually found, as you know. But me?" He shook his head. "They're still beating the bushes for me, I'm afraid." He looked out the window at the sideview mirror again. "Hell, those dimwits couldn't find water if they fell out of a boat. You take the way they were looking for Bettis, for example. They staked out his house and the shoe store where he worked, and that was it. They just sat there and waited for him to show up. They followed his wife around, yeah—any fool would've known to do that—but they never put a tail on anybody else. And you wanna know why that was a mistake? Because when a man's in trouble, Mrs. Loudermilk, he doesn't always look to his wife for help first. He goes to his *friends*. Somebody he can trust, who'll do whatever he needs done without asking a million and one questions first. You see what I'm saying?

"That's why, while the Feds were tailing the wife, I was tailing the other salesman at the shoe store. Bettis's co-worker."

"Bob," I said.

"Yeah. Bob. How'd you know that?" He waved me off before I could answer. "Never mind. I forgot, you're the curious type. Sooner or later, people like you know everything, right?

"Anyway, I followed this Bob around for two days, and bingo, it paid off. He goes out for lunch on the second day and leads me right to Bettis. The two of 'em meet in a supermarket parking lot out on the east side of town and he gives Bettis a couple of dollars and sends

him on his way. Bettis never even got out of the car—
he just took the money and drove off. I go to follow
him, and the heap I'm driving stalls out. Right there in
the parking lot, a brand-new Caddy, it goes fifteen feet
and dies, just like that, as Bettis gets away. Last goddamn Cadillac *I'll* ever lift in a pinch, I can promise you
that. Anyway—''

"Where are we going?" I asked him abruptly, tired
of driving blind to what, in all probability, was going to
be my own funeral.

"When we get there, I'll tell you," Gottifucci said,
irritated. "Now, do you wanna hear this story, or not?"

"I want to know where we're going."

"I don't know where we're going, yet. An appropriate
place to pull over, that's all I can tell you, all right?"

"Appropriate for what?"

Gottifucci hesitated for a moment, then set his jaw
and answered the question. "Appropriate for the accident you're gonna have," he said. "Are you happy
now?"

I bit my tongue and just nodded at him.

"All right then. Where the hell was I?"

"The Cadillac broke down on you," I said, sorry we
had ever gotten off the subject in the first place.

"Oh yeah. The Caddy. So Bettis gets away, right?
And from the looks of it, he's gone for good. Only way
I can think of to find out where he's gone is to ask his
buddy the shoe salesman. Bob. I know his name's Bob
because I heard Bettis call him that that first day in the
store. I let him get back to work, and then I give him a
call, tell him I'm with the FBI and that we know he just

saw Bettis. 'Tell us where your friend Geoffry went when he left you a few minutes ago, and we might decide not to arrest you,' I say. Very polite, very cordial. 'The Grand Canyon,' he says, without so much as a moment's hesitation. 'He went to the Grand Canyon.'

"*The Grand Canyon? I say to myself. What the hell does he wanna go to the Grand Canyon for?* But I don't bother asking Bob that question, because I know he isn't going to know the answer. The jerk knows too much already, Bettis isn't gonna tell him all his business, right? So I just go out there. I hang up the phone, find me another car, and drive up to the Grand Canyon."

"And that's where you killed him."

"You have to understand, Mrs. Loudermilk. The little weasel was going to turn me over to my friends back in Baltimore. It was him or me, simple as that."

"But why did you have to do it in our trailer? Couldn't you have found a more appropriate place to . . . to . . ."

"Knock him off? Sure, I could have. And I wanted to. But he never gave me the chance. Less than an hour after I found him up there, he caught me in a restaurant giving him the eye and recognized me right away. Next thing I know, I'm chasing him into the trailer park, and watching him duck into your trailer. He didn't think I saw him, but I did.

"Well, I go in after him and find him sitting on the can, shaking like a leaf. I tell him, 'Pull your pants down, Geoffry, make yourself comfortable,' and start laughing like hell when he does like I say. Then I make him tell me what he's doing up there. He says he's got a meeting scheduled with somebody representing the Caprice brothers at one o'clock, they're gonna give him a half a million for the pictures he took of me, and for the address where they were taken. Only he hasn't got the pictures on him. And he refuses to tell me where they are.'' He shrugged. ''So I shot him. He didn't think I would, but I did. I figured if *I* couldn't find the goddamn pictures, neither would the Caprice gorillas. Right? They're gonna travel all that way and have nothing to show for it but the memory of seeing some dead guy sitting on the toilet.'' He chuckled heartily, like a barfly recalling the punch line of a particularly funny joke. ''So I just gave him a quick pat-down and got the hell out of there. I didn't think he'd had time to stash anything in the trailer, so I figured maybe the stuff was in his car. Only his car was empty when I found it a few minutes later where he'd parked it—there was nothing in it but some junk in the glove compartment and some trash all over the floor and on the seats. I looked all over that car, then I just gave up and left. I must've been halfway back to Flagstaff when I realized I'd left the gun I used on Bettis under the goddamn passenger seat.''

He shook his head to scold himself. ''Fortunately, my prints weren't anywhere on it, so there was no real harm done.''

''Except to the man they're holding in jail back in Flagstaff, you mean,'' I said, scowling.

''Oh, yeah. Him.'' Gottifucci eyed the Ford's speedometer critically. ''Watch your speed there, Mrs. L. And keep your eyes on the road, please.''

I turned around and eased up on the gas, slowing our pace by about five miles an hour to an even sixty.

"Some loser, huh? He goes up to the Canyon to get himself a getaway car, and he takes Bettis's. The one car in the whole place that can pin a murder rap on him. Jesus." He shook his head again.

"So why are you still here?" I asked him. "You'd made a clean getaway. Why aren't you out in Florida, or Mexico, or maybe even up in Canada somewhere, by now?"

"Because," he said, "I can't. I *can't*. I wish to hell I could, but there's just no way. Without the Feds to protect me, I wouldn't last a week. Anywhere. I know it, and they know it."

"But you've committed a murder. A murder they didn't sanction. Surely they won't continue to protect you after *this*."

"You don't think so, huh? Wake up and smell the coffee, Mrs. Loudermilk. The FBI and I made a deal. And if there's one thing the fucking Feds are good for, it's holding up their end of a deal. *Any* deal. They're sort of like Boy Scouts in that respect. Very loyal. Very dependable." He turned to take a look at the road, and his eyes flew open like they'd seen a ghost: *"Look out!"*

Somebody had dropped the jagged remains of a rusted tail pipe in the middle of our lane, and I rolled right over it. I'd had my eyes on Gottifucci instead of where we were going, and I hadn't seen it coming. I tried to steer around it when he screamed, but I knew better than to try too hard; yank the wheel too fast with eight thousand pounds of trailer tied to your flank, and you'll both end up doing more flips across the highway than an Olympic gymnast might do during floor exercises. In the end, all I was able to do was spare Lucille; she straddled the serrated metal snake perfectly and was never touched. But our pickup had taken the twisted metal husk head-on, and lost; the sound of at least one of its tires blowing had been nearly deafening.

"I oughta kill you for that," Gottifucci snapped as I brought the limping Ford and Lucille to a stop on the highway's shoulder. "I told you to keep an eye on the road!"

"It was an accident!" I said, watching and waiting for the gun in his hand to fire.

He didn't say anything for a long time, trying to decide what to do. Finally, he brushed a few wayward strands of hair from his face with his free hand and said, "All right, out. This way." He opened the door on his side to back slowly out of the truck, and I followed after him. Once outside, he pulled me close, stuck the gun up against my hip, and together we surveyed the damage: one flat and shredded tire, passenger side rear.

"Shit," Gottifucci said.

"What the hell happened?" Big Joe suddenly demanded. He had thrown Lucille's door open and jumped down out of the trailer, and now he was moving toward us. Bad Dog was right behind him, matching him step for step.

"Nothing! Get the hell back in there, now!" Gottifucci cried, turning me around so my husband could get a good look at the gun pressed hard against my side.

"I ran over something in the road and blew a tire, baby, that's all," I said.

"A tire? Where?"

"I thought I told you to get back inside!" Gottifucci screamed.

"On the truck," I said to Joe. "This one over here, in the rear."

"I'm gonna give you five seconds, Mr. Loudermilk," Gottifucci said. "One—"

"Okay, okay," Joe said, holding his hands up in a placating manner. "You don't want that tire changed, fine. State trooper'll be along in a minute or two, you can ask him to do it for you."

"To hell with that. Your wife'll change it."

"Oh no I won't," I said. "I can't!"

"What do you mean, you can't?"

"She means that in order to change a flat on the rear end of that truck, this trailer's gotta be unhitched first," Joe said. "And she doesn't know the first thing about doing that. Do you, baby?"

I shook my head.

"What about him?" Gottifucci asked, referring to Bad Dog.

Dog shook *his* head.

"Look. It's real simple," Joe said. "You want that tire changed, you're gonna have to let me unhitch this trailer. Fast. Otherwise, we're gonna be here awhile. Just asking for company. Is that what you want?"

Gottifucci fell silent, thinking. I could hear his breathing change rhythm as he watched the cars whiz by us on both sides of the highway—waiting, I supposed, for one of them to be the state trooper sedan that Joe had so deftly placed in his mind.

"Okay. Go ahead," Gottifucci said in time. "Do what you have to do, and get it over with. But remember one thing: You try anything smart, and your wife is dead. You hear me?"

Joe nodded his head solemnly. "I hear you."

As Joe went quickly to work, Bad Dog approached Gottifucci and asked, "Okay if I watch?" He sounded like a six-year-old asking his mother if he could lick the cake spoon.

"Knock yourself out," Gottifucci said.

And that was how it went, Joe laboring while the rest of us watched, four actors in a little sideshow playing along the southbound shoulder of Interstate 17. As Bad Dog knelt beside his father, Gottifucci and I stood nearby, dividing our attention between Joe and the flow of traffic that kept threatening to blow us off our feet. We were looking for state trooper patrol cars, though neither one of us wanted to see one—Gottifucci for obvious reasons, and me because I didn't think I'd care for Gottifucci's reaction to one. His gun, though invisible to anyone on the highway, was still being jammed firmly into my side, a constant reminder that death was only as far away as he chose to hold it.

Fifteen minutes crawled by, and Gottifucci was getting crazy. Big Joe had Lucille unhitched, but he was just now positioning the jack under the rear end of our pickup.

"Hurry it up!" Gottifucci snapped at him.

"I'm doing the best I can," Joe said.

And then we all heard it: the distinct sound of gravel popping. The four of us turned toward it just in time to see the red Chevy truck slide to a halt along the shoulder of the road, right behind Lucille.

"Oh my God," I said.

There was an Airstream trailer hitched to the rear of the Chevy; an old twenty-six-foot International, from the looks of it. Sunlight was flashing off its silver skin like white lightning.

"Friends of yours?" Gottifucci asked me, as the driver's-side door of the Chevy swung open.

"I don't think so. But it's hard to tell from here."

"Doesn't matter." He glanced over at Joe and Dog as they stepped up alongside us to see who our visitor was. "You're gonna get rid of 'em, whoever they are. Fast. Otherwise, it's shoot-'em-up time." He gave them a fresh but discreet look at the gun he had pressed to my back.

"You don't know what these people are like," I said. "They see another Airstreamer in trouble—"

It was all I had time to say, for the Chevy's driver, a red-bearded bear of a man in a green plaid shirt and faded denim pants, was suddenly upon us. He didn't look the least bit familiar to me, but he was smiling at all four of us as if we were old friends.

"Howdy, folks. Havin' a little trouble, are you?"

I waited to see if Gottifucci wanted to answer that, but he didn't, so I said, "We just had a flat. My husband's taking care of it."

"I see." He turned to Joe. "Anything I can do to

help? The wife an' I are always ready to lend a hand, we see another Airstreamer pulled up lame.''

"No thanks," Joe said, stone-faced and emotionless.

"You sure? Anything you need, we'd be glad to help. How about some cold drinks for the ladies here? We've got plenty in the truck." He was looking right at Gottifucci and me now, trying to be charming. If he could see through Gottifucci's disguise, his face didn't betray it; if anything, in fact, he looked rather enamored of him.

"Thank you, no," I said.

"All right. My name's Rick Glanville, by the way. But my friends call me Rusty." He held out his hand for Joe to shake, and my husband took it grudgingly. "That's my wife, Kitty, in the truck back there. I don't know if you can see her too well from here, though."

"Look, Mr. Glanville—" I started to say.

"So. How do you like your Excella? Or is that a stupid question?" Glanville was giving Lucille the once-over, his lust for her written all over his face.

"It's a load of crap," Big Joe said sharply, and my eyes nearly rolled up into my head.

"How's that again?" Glanville asked, turning.

"I said, it's a load of crap. A pile of junk. Worst excuse for a trailer on the road."

"You mean you got a lemon?"

"I mean that I should've bought a Winnebago. That's what I mean."

"A *Winnebago?*"

"You heard me. I wouldn't buy another Airstream if my life depended on it."

Glanville couldn't believe his ears. "Now, waitaminute, partner . . ." he said.

"Waitaminute, nothin'. They're junk, all of 'em, and anybody dumb enough to own one deserves all the grief they get. Now, if you don't mind, we've got work to do, like my wife said. But thanks for stoppin' by."

Glanville was furious; not a trace of his down-home good humor was left to be seen on his face. "Okay," he said to Joe, nodding his head up and down. "I don't know what your problem is, buddy, but if that's how you want it, I'm gone. But you better know one little thing before I go—" He pointed an angry finger directly at my husband's nose. "The Wally Byam Caravan Club is gonna hear about this, and when they do, you folks better never, *ever* let anybody catch you at one of our rallies. You got that?"

Calm as you please, Joe took three giant steps forward to bring himself within an inch of Glanville's freckled face. "Wally Byam was a *punk,*" he said, poking his right index finger into the large man's chest to accentuate the word "punk."

Then he ducked.

The punch Glanville threw with his right hand hit Gottifucci flush on the nose, hard, and Gottifucci had never for a moment seen it coming. Joe had positioned himself perfectly to ensure that he wouldn't. I heard the blow connect, and afterward felt, more than saw, the oddly dressed man behind me crumple to the ground, falling as if someone had tossed him a medicine ball before cutting him down at the knees. Somewhere on

the way down, he and his wig parted ways, so that Glanville had a big surprise coming when he peered down at
the body to assess the damage he had done.

"Aw, hell," was all he said.

____ 12 __

"We let things get out of control. I'm sorry," Agent Medavoy said.

It wasn't the first time he had said it. Ever since his arrival at the tiny sheriff's office in Bumble Bee, Arizona, where we had all been taken to issue our statements, he had been offering the same apology. To me, to Joe, even to Bad Dog. It seemed genuine enough, but that didn't mean it was worth anything; maybe a cup of coffee, at the most.

Gottifucci had implied that the FBI was committed to covering for him, no matter how many bodies he piled up in the interests of "self-preservation," but Medavoy denied it. He said the Bureau would have stepped in themselves to save us from Gottifucci had they only known where to find him. I wanted to believe that, but I wasn't sure I could.

"We could have been killed," I'd say to Medavoy.

"Yes ma'am," he'd say to me. "But if you'd been honest with us . . ."

And so it went, around and around and around. The truth was, we had all messed up, playing our games of secrets and lies, and it was only by the grace of God that our foolishness had not resulted in anyone's untimely demise. Or incarceration. We all knew good and well that Medavoy had the option of tossing us in jail and throwing away the key, so numerous were the charges he could have leveled against us, but that would have made for a very noisy end to the Gottifucci episode, from his vantage point, and noise was not generally what the FBI liked best. What they liked was quiet, especially when the alternative would almost certainly bring them considerable public embarrassment. It was no wonder, then, that Medavoy ultimately offered us a deal that we anxiously accepted: our silence for his forgiveness.

Freedom of expression wasn't much to give up when you were just glad to be alive, and we were only alive, Bad Dog and I knew, because of Big Joe. To save our bacon, he had gone the extra mile, saying terrible, unthinkable things about his beloved Airstream brand so that a prideful Rusty Glanville might take a poke at him. It had been quick thinking on Joe's part, and everyone had told him so, even Danny Gottifucci before they led him away. Joe didn't want to hear it, but I told him he had only proved all over again that he still had it, that "Inspector Loudermilk" magic. Once a cop, always a cop, is the way Bad Dog put it.

Joe told him to shut up.

We spent that Saturday night at a Comfort Inn in Phoenix, but not before Joe and Rusty Glanville had swapped a few war stories over a six-pack of beer and threatened to be friends for life. Two men with absolutely nothing in common save for their unyielding infatuation with Airstreams. Glanville's wife, Kitty, and I both knew that would be more than enough to bond them together forever; we'd each seen it happen before, time and time again. Kitty said if Churchill and Hitler had owned Airstreams, there would have never been a Second World War. I told her I didn't doubt it for a minute.

I put Joe to bed early that night, and tried to do the same for myself, but sleep just wouldn't find me. Too much had happened too fast over the last five days, and now that it was over, closing my eyes only brought it all rushing back to me, one bad scene after another. Giving up somewhere shortly after nine, I left the bedroom to see if Dog had any interest in playing a few games of gin rummy, but he was gone. The foldout bed we had left him in at the front of our hotel room was empty; the TV was on, but the sound had been muted.

Our last night together, and he was out fooling around.

At least, that was my first thought, until my maternal instincts took over and I began to worry about him in earnest. Not for his safety, mind you, but for his emotional well-being. His soul, his spirit. His *heart*.

You'd have to be a mother to understand.

Mothers know things. They can *sense* things. And nine times out of ten, they can find their missing children in the first place they look, just as I found my son less than a half hour later: out in the hotel parking lot, inside Lucille. Asleep.

"How'd you know I was out here?" he asked me when I stirred him awake. He'd been stretched out on our bed, shoes all over the bedspread.

Rather than work the Powers of Mom angle on him, I just said, "Your father's keys were missing."

"Oh." He rubbed his eyes with both hands.

"Theodore, what are you doing out here?"

"I don't know." He shrugged. "I just . . . wanted to spend a little time in here, I guess. Before I leave, I mean." He looked up into my face, searching for the right words. "It's like, this is your home now, Moms. Right? This is my *parents' home*. And . . ." He shrugged again. "It feels good to be here, that's all. It feels *good*. So, I thought I'd hang out a little, while I could. While there's still time."

He threw himself into my arms. "I love you, Moms. Pops too."

It was one of those moments your kids count on to purchase them a little absolution. They think they can bribe you with five minutes of genuine emotion, one thin little sliver of remorse and/or gratitude, and all the grief they've ever laid at your doorstep will be erased from the ledger like a mere accountant's error. They think if they show you the babies you once held in your arms for just one fleeting moment, you'll forget what those babies have become and lay down your life for them, again and again and again.

They are so right.

"We love you, too, Theodore," I said.

And then we played some cards.

The next day, Sunday, we didn't leave our room to take Dog to the Greyhound station until well after check-out time. I'll bet you'd never guess why.

Final score: Los Angeles Raiders 24, Pittsburgh Steelers 13. Dozer Meadows didn't play, as expected, but he could be seen on TV waving a towel on the Raider sideline every time the Silver and Black did something right, which was apparently often.

Yeah, I know, girls. I was thinking the same thing the entire game.

Jeez Looweez.

Here's a special excerpt from the next
Gar Anthony Haywood mystery
featuring Joe and Dottie Loudermilk . . .

BAD NEWS TRAVELS FAST

. . . available in hardcover from Putnam

Lincoln's eyes moved.

At least, that was what the crazy woman doing all the shouting was insisting. "I saw his eyes move! He looked right at me! I saw his eyes move!" she screamed, moving from tourist to tourist like a hummingbird flitting from chrysanthemum to chrysanthemum, trying to get people to look. Those that humored her were disappointed, of course; the huge stone centerpiece of the Lincoln Memorial remained unfazed, eyes fixed as firmly and implacably on the crystalline pool facing the monument as they had been since its opening in 1922.

The crazy woman's husband, meanwhile, was mortified. They were both too old for this. She was creating an incredible scene, and all eyes (other than Abraham Lincoln's, unfortunately) were on his wife. They had traveled hundreds of miles to visit Washington, D.C., fulfilling one of his lifelong dreams, and this, no doubt, was going to be the highlight of their trip: being fitted for straight jackets on the steps of the Lincoln Memorial on a sun-drenched August afternoon.

"I saw his eyes move! Really! They looked right at me!"

She was now yanking on the sleeve of a tall, square-jawed fellow in a Washington Redskins warm-up jacket, trying to pull him closer to the giant statue. He wasn't budging.

Her husband tried to break her grip on the poor man, but couldn't. He was aware now that people had finally connected them as a couple, and were waiting for him to assert some authority and take charge of the situation.

They didn't know his wife very well.

Inevitably, one of the Memorial's security guards came over to try to rein in the madwoman himself, but he only ended up chasing her about like a cowboy trying to rope a calf. The crowd roared. The husband moaned. A second security guard joined in the chase to heighten the hilarity. It all made for a free show no one expected to get, but all were overjoyed to receive.

Finally, two uniformed police officers appeared out of nowhere to break things up. They sliced through the crowd expertly and took the hysterical woman into custody with surprisingly little muss or fuss. The mere sight of them seemed to take all the fight out of her.

"Take it easy now, ma'am," one of them said as they put the handcuffs on her. "Everything's going to be okay."

"But I saw his eyes move," I told them, making the claim one last time just for effect.

The two officers just nodded their heads and walked me gingerly down the Memorial's steps to their waiting police car.

Following close behind, I heard my humiliated husband mumble something quietly under his breath.

"Jeez Looweez," he said.

_____ 1 __

But I'm getting ahead of myself.

Stories are meant to be told from the beginning, not from somewhere near the end. And the beginning of this story comes four days before the "Psycho Grandma on Drugs Visits the Lincoln Memorial" episode I've just described.

So let me back up a little.

I went bonkers at the feet of Honest Abe on a Friday. The previous Monday, my husband, Big Joe, and I were on the road, headed north on Interstate 95 in Virginia, less than thirty miles south of the nation's capital. We were on the road because that's where the two of us live now, on the road. We're what are known in some circles as "full-timers"; globe-trotting trailer-home owners with no permanent address.

People become full-timers for many different reasons, but Joe and I have more reasons than most. Five, to be exact. The names of these five reasons are Maureen, De-lila, Walter, Edward, and Theodore. These are our children, as you may have already guessed. Grown children, by chronological standards, but hardly out of puberty in terms of emotional maturity. In fact, with the lone exception of Maureen (whom we all refer to as "Mo"), these five individuals are the most consistently annoying human beings on this earth. They go to school, but take pains not to learn anything remotely useful; they seek and find employment, only to see who can be shown the door the fastest. They date weird people and adhere to Mickey Mouse religions. They give birth to grandchildren from hell and raise them like pet goldfish they won at a church carnival. And they borrow money from their parents the way some European nations borrow from the U.S. government: by the trillions. Only the Defense Department spends money faster.

So when the time came for Joe and me to retire early—him from the El Segundo, California, Police Department, and me from the faculty of Loyola Marymount University—the question wasn't how often we'd like to leave home, but how fast could we get out of town, and where could we best hide for the remainder of our lives. As things turned out, the answer to the first question was, as fast as we could sell our home (three months), and the answer to the second, nowhere and everywhere. Home for Joe and Dottie Loudermilk now is the open highway, and while that has taken some getting used to, it has had the desired effects of making us almost impossible to find when a) Delila wants to introduce us to her latest psychotic husband; b) Walter needs investors for his partner's waterless Jacuzzi; c) Theodore has to sell a hundred and fifty boxes of Afrocentric Hanukkah cards in mid-June to avoid another lawsuit; or d) Edward is looking for a place to lie low so as to avoid running into one knife-wielding ex-girlfriend or another.

If you're beginning to feel an ulcer coming on just listening to this, I believe I've made my point.

They're our kids, and we love them, but Joe and I figured we could love them just as well from a distance of several hundred miles as we could from our old living room, and at far less expense. Hence, the ink wasn't dry on our retirement questionnaires when we hit the ground running and told Mo, our newly elected financial manager-slash-family liaison, "Don't call us, we'll call you."

That was almost two years ago.

Since that time, Big Joe and I have put over forty-five thousand miles on our Ford Lightning pickup and twenty-seven-foot Airstream trailer home, hopping from one resort city or state park to the next, with no discernible method to our madness. We go where our collective whim takes us, and we stay as long as we like. It's a great life for two old geezers in their mid-fifties; every day is different, every day brings something new.

And none of our heartbreaking, debt-inducing kids are around to spoil the fun.

Usually.

I mean, we have on a few rare occasions crossed paths with one or two of our children, but not because we ever planned it that way. We just accidentally ran into the child, or fell victim to some unfortunate breach of security that enabled him or her to track us down like a pair of escaped killers last seen on *America's Most Wanted*. After all the trouble and expense we've gone to to avoid any further contact with our unholy offspring, it would be criminal for one of us to actually arrange a rendezvous with one of them. Absolutely criminal.

Which is why I've only done it once, up to now.

"Did you say 'Eddie'?" Big Joe asked. This was on a Monday, if you recall what I said earlier. Out on Interstate 95, thirty miles shy of Washington, D.C.

"Yes," I said.

"*Our* Eddie?"

"Our son Eddie, yes."

"And you said—"

"That we'll be meeting him for dinner tonight. Yes."

He hadn't taken his eyes off the road yet, and that worried me.

"Says who?" he finally asked, turning. I imagined an egg on the top of his beautifully bald brown head, frying sunnyside-up with a snap, crackle, and pop of bacon grease.

"Joe, we are not going to argue about this," I said flatly.

"You're darn right we're not."

"Joe—"

"That boy is a lost cause, Dottie. He's over the edge."

"Just because his politics don't agree with ours—"

"You call it politics. I call it psycho-babble. Anti-American psycho-babble."

"Joe, he is *not* anti-American. He just . . . happens to see America a little differently than most people, that's all."

Joe cocked his head at me and raised an eyebrow, declining to even dignify my statement with a retort.

Saying our son Eddie saw America a little differently than most folks was like saying the Beatles once had a somewhat different view of haircuts than most ex-Marines. The truth was, Eddie was an extremist where his politics were concerned, to the extent that he saw a government conspiracy around every corner. If the phone company had made a mistake on his bill, it was because the FBI had tapped into the phone company's computer and fouled things up trying to trace and/or monitor his calls. If his cable company lost its C-SPAN signal for more than six minutes, it was proof that Congress didn't want the average American to know what kind of corrupt business it was cooking up next. Joe liked to say the boy couldn't lick a stamp for fear the U.S. Postal Service was poisoning the glue—and I had to admit, that was only a slight exaggeration.

"All right," I said finally. "So he does have a screw or two loose, in some ways. I'll grant you that. But that doesn't mean we can't sit down and have a meal with the child, does it?"

"What's he doing in Washington? Did you ask him that?"

"He said he was here with some friends. They've formed some kind of political-action committee."

"Uh-huh." Joe was nodding his head at the road ahead, congratulating himself for having predicted I would say something along those lines.

"They're here to lobby against some bill, Joe. Not blowing up the Washington Monument."

"That's how they all get started, terrorists. 'Lobbying.' One minute they're passing out leaflets, and the next they're chucking grenades.''

"Oh, don't be ridiculous . . . ''

"Ridiculous?''

"Yes, ridiculous. The boy may be spacey, but he isn't insane.''

"Well, call it what you will. Whatever Eddie's condition is, it makes for lousy dinner conversation, and I'm in no mood to hear it. All right?''

"Joe—''

"I said, forget it. You just call that boy the minute we get to the trailer park and tell him we can't make it. We'll catch him at Mo's this Thanksgiving, or Christmas, or whenever.''

When I didn't answer that, he turned again to face me, determined to both see and hear me acquiesce.

"Whatever you say, baby,'' I said.

Thirty-one years I've been using that line, and he still thinks it means "Okay.''